THE RAGGED SEAMSTRESS

Victorian Romance

FAYE GODWIN

Tica House Publishing

Sweet Romance that Delights and Enchants!

Copyright © 2022 by Faye Godwin

All rights reserved.

No part of this book may be reproduced in any form or by any electronic or mechanical means, including information storage and retrieval systems, without written permission from the author, except for the use of brief quotations in a book review.

PERSONAL WORD FROM THE AUTHOR

Dearest Readers,

I'm so delighted that you have chosen one of my books to read. I am proud to be a part of the team of writers at Tica House Publishing. Our goal is to inspire, entertain, and give you many hours of reading pleasure. Your kind words and loving readership are deeply appreciated.

I would like to personally invite you to sign up for updates and to become part of our **Exclusive Reader Club**—it's completely Free to Join! I'd love to welcome you!

Much love,

Faye Godwin

FAYE GODWIN

CLICK HERE to Join our Reader's Club and to Receive Tica House Updates!

https://victorian.subscribemenow.com/

CONTENTS

Personal Word From The Author — 1

PART I
Chapter 1 — 7
Chapter 2 — 21

PART II
Chapter 3 — 29
Chapter 4 — 50
Chapter 5 — 64

PART III
Chapter 6 — 93
Chapter 7 — 101
Chapter 8 — 110
Chapter 9 — 117
Chapter 10 — 130
Chapter 11 — 141

PART IV
Chapter 12 — 149
Chapter 13 — 160
Chapter 14 — 171
Chapter 15 — 184

PART V
Chapter 16 — 197
Chapter 17 — 207
Chapter 18 — 216
Chapter 19 — 231

Chapter 20	244
Chapter 21	259

PART VI
Chapter 22	269
Chapter 23	275
Epilogue	285
Continue Reading...	290
Thanks For Reading	293
More Faye Godwin Victorian Romances!	295
About the Author	297

PART I

CHAPTER 1

BLANCHE EPLETT WORKED the duster over the figurines on the mantelpiece in careful circles, whisking aside the tiny specks of dust that had gathered in the single day since the last time she'd carefully cleaned every corner of the study. She blew at a stray strand of hair that trickled down her face, then reached up and tucked it back under her bonnet before resuming her work. It was early afternoon, and she'd already worked nine hours, and she had another five or six to look forward to before her day was done. Her hands cramped, her back ached, and she wanted nothing more than to rest.

But she knew the Turners placed great value on these little trinkets, knew it from conversations she'd overheard while she was at work. The little ceramic elephant – the colourful one – had come all the way from India, where the original Ludwig Turner had first made his fortune generations ago.

There was a glass case holding a series of war medals. None of them belonged to the current Mr. Turner (Ludwig the third, Blanche believed). Instead, his was the photograph in the frame that glared sternly out at her as she ran her duster over the glass.

She couldn't keep herself from hesitating a moment, running the cloth a second time over the glass, admiring the fine, strong lines of Mr. Turner's jaw and the piercing, noble expression in his eyes. The photograph had captured the fierceness in him, the sharp slant of his eyebrows, the height and definition of his cheekbones. But it had not been able to portray the other things about Mr. Turner that always made Blanche's heart flutter: the deep baritone of his voice, which always sounded as though at any moment he might break into laughter or song; the piercing green of his eyes, sharp and clear and yet somehow mysterious at the same time.

She was polishing the photograph a third time, unnecessarily, when she heard the creak of the study door. Starting guiltily, Blanche hurried to carry on dusting the mantelpiece. Not only was Mr. Turner the master of a fine household and she a mere housemaid, one whom he likely didn't even know existed, but he was married, too. He may as well have lived on the moon for all the access she might have had to him, no matter how his photograph made her feel.

"I'm nearly done here, Mrs. Boswick," she said quickly, knowing it must be the housekeeper come to check up on her. "I'll finish before Mr. Turner comes home."

"I'm afraid it's rather too late for that," said a warm baritone, smooth as silk against her skin.

Blanche whirled around, clutching the duster to her chest, a strange burst of both panic and elation running through her body. Mr. Turner himself was standing in the doorway, his hands buried in the pockets of his elegantly cut tweed shooting-jacket. He must be fresh from shooting pheasants with his friends; his boots were muddy, his wonderful chocolate-dark hair in disarray, and a fragrance of open air and heather emanated from him. It was all more enchanting than Blanche could express. She wrung the duster in her hands as though she could wring the feelings clean out of herself.

"I'm s-sorry, Mr. Turner, sir," she said, dropping her eyes to the ground, forcing them not to linger on Mr. Turner's intense gaze. She could still feel it on her, warming her skin like firelight. "I'm all done here." She frantically started to gather up her things into her basket, mortified at what Mrs. Boswick would say if she found out about Blanche's latest failure.

"Oh, I don't mind," said Mr. Turner. He strode over to the drink cabinet by the desk and Blanche heard tumblers and flasks clinking, then the slosh of liquid.

She thought it strange, then, that Mr. Turner had come down to the study, so muddy and tired from hunting. Normally he would change at once, perhaps have a meal, before retiring to the study to smoke and read. Still, it was none of her business what any of these rich folk did. Ever since she'd been purchased from the workhouse four years ago, Blanche had been determined to keep her head down and retain her job.

Mr. Turner swallowed, smacking his lips appreciatively. "Has Mrs. Turner come back from her visit to her... friend, in Piccadilly?" he asked.

"I – I've not seen her, sir," said Blanche. "I don't think so."

"Neither do I. She always stays long." Mr. Turner sighed. "Your name is Blanche, isn't it?"

Blanche felt a ripple of shock, and simultaneously, a ripple of pleasure at the sound of her name. "Yes, sir."

"You know, Blanche," said Mr. Turner quietly, "sometimes I do envy people of low estate, like you. Your lives must be so much simpler. Especially your marriages."

"I wouldn't know, sir," said Blanche. She'd gathered the last of her things, but when she turned toward the doorway, he was standing in her way, watching her. There was something in the way his eyes travelled over her and the way his lip quirked up in a smile that sent a delicious chill across her whole body.

"So, you're not married?" he asked.

"No, sir," said Blanche. "If you could excuse me, sir..."

"I am married," said Mr. Turner, ignoring her. "More's the pity, too. I never loved Camellia, you know. I can hardly blame her for seeking solace in another man's arms." He took another swig of the whisky.

Blanche shifted her weight. "I'm sorry, sir," she said, moving toward the door, "but I really must..."

Then he reached out, grabbing her arm, quickly but not roughly, and when Blanche looked up at him this time his face was very close to hers. She could still smell the heather on his clothes, the expensive, smoky whisky on his breath, and his eyes searched hers in a way that made goosebumps rise on her skin.

"I've been watching you, Blanche," he whispered. "I've been watching you a long time."

The words felt like something out of a secret fantasy, out of some whimsical dream that Blanche had never allowed herself to truly think of. She hadn't known how long she had been wishing for those words until she heard them. Suddenly she couldn't look away from his eyes; she felt captivated by him, magnetized, irresistibly drawn.

Mr. Turner leaned down and kissed her, once, very gently, his lips finding hers, caressing them softly, then pulling away. Blanche found herself leaning after him. Her heart and mind were crying out that this was wrong, horribly, horribly wrong. But her body cried out for more. Much more.

Mr. Turner looked into her eyes for a few long seconds, as though gauging her reaction. When she leaned up against him, her basket falling from numb fingers, he did not hesitate. His hands found her shoulders, her neck, her face. He pulled her closer, and she melted into him, and he was kissing her mouth and her cheeks and her neck and –

AT THE DOCTOR'S WORDS, Blanche's hands fluttered at once to her stomach. Moments ago, it had still felt flat and tiny, scooped out and hollowed by a life of hard labour and basic food. But now she fancied she could already feel a difference, already feel a curve growing there, something illicit and dreadful, something life changing. It felt as though the floor was tipping out from under her, threatening to send her plunging headfirst into a sea of ice.

"Are you sure?" she gasped. "Can you be sure?"

The doctor gave her a grim look, his grey eyes filled with judgment that pelted her skin like stones.

"I am absolutely sure," he said coldly. "That will be two shillings."

The sum was unthinkable, but Blanche couldn't think at that moment. She fumbled the coins from her purse, even though they represented almost all the money she had earned in the past week and staggered out into the street.

When the vomiting had started, the fainting, the dizziness, she'd feared the same cancer that had taken her mother from her and had sent her into the workhouse when she was only five years old. But this was almost worse. Cancer could kill her.

This could destroy her life.

Her feet carried her back to the Turner house, because there was nowhere else to go, although it felt like she was seeing the world from inside a glass bubble. As though she was floating, untethered, in a hostile world that would no longer recognize her as one of its own. It was a Sunday afternoon, and Mrs. Turner was taking a stroll outside among the flowers on the arm of her lady's maid. From behind a hedge, Blanche watched.

Mrs. Turner's belly was round and swollen; it would be their fourth child. Suddenly, Blanche felt filthy, the weight of what she'd done surrounding her with an awful force that made her gasp and press her hands over her mouth. Ludwig was married. His wife was pregnant.

How could she have allowed this to happen?

Tears coursed down Blanche's cheeks, and she staggered toward the servants' quarters, sobs clutching at her chest. She was alone – no. She was not alone, not anymore, and she had a tiny life to care for now, but soon she would have no job and no prospects, and she would starve, and so would her baby, Ludwig's baby –

"Blanche?"

Blanche stumbled to a halt, whipping around. Ludwig Turner was standing in the archway to the rose garden, his brows knitted in puzzlement, and she suddenly remembered then that they had planned their next secret rendezvous for Sunday afternoon in the rose garden. It was overgrown, and they had enjoyed many an afternoon on the cool grass beneath the bushes.

Many an afternoon that had led to this.

Terror lanced through Blanche, and she backed away, ready to run.

"Blanche, my darling, my beauty." Ludwig reached out, grasping her hands. "What on Earth is the matter? Why are you in tears?"

"Please let me go," Blanche sobbed, tugging at her hands. "Please just let me go."

"But my sweet, my angel, what's happened? Who's done this to you?" Darkness brooded in Ludwig's eyes. "Tell me, and I'll put it right. Whatever it is, let me fix it."

"There's no fixing this, Ludwig." Blanche sobbed out, doubling over with the force of her grief and terror. "I'm – ruined. Ruined."

"You could never be ruined, not with me to care for you, my love," said Ludwig. He pulled her closer, planted one of his most delicate kisses on her forehead, his thumbs gently caressing the backs of her hands. "Just tell me... tell me... whatever it is, I'll help you. I promise."

Blanche couldn't keep the words bottled inside her anymore. She knew he had to find out at some point, and that she couldn't keep secrets from him – from everyone else in the world, yes, but not from him.

"I'm pregnant," she cried out. "I'm pregnant with your child."

Ludwig's grip wobbled on her hands, and she kept her head bowed, terrified of seeing his face, of the scolding she would receive for her carelessness.

Instead, his voice was a quaver. "You – you are?"

"Yes," she sobbed out. "Ludwig, I'm sorry. Please don't punish me. I'm so, so sorry."

His hands tightened on hers then. "But Blanche," he said, "I'm not."

His voice bubbled with the last emotion Blanche had been expecting: excitement. She raised her head, and inexplicably it was in his eyes as well.

"What?" she stammered.

"Oh, Blanche, darling, this is almost as good as being able to get married." Ludwig beamed down at her. "We're having a baby."

"But it – it won't be – legitimate," Blanche choked out.

"I know the rest of the world cares about that, but I don't. I just want you to be happy." Ludwig squeezed her hands. "Don't you worry about a thing, my love. I can't wait to meet our child."

Blanche stared up into his eyes, her heart thudding in her chest, feeling a flow of something warm and glorious rush through her – relief mixed with something far deeper: love. When Ludwig had first cornered her that night in his study, she had dared only to believe he was as attracted to her as she was attracted to him. But even through all this time, she had only ever thought of herself as his plaything, had only ever considered that his interest in her could never equal her real and abiding love for him. How could it be otherwise? He was married.

Married, and yet she was carrying his baby, the half-sibling of those children playing outside with Mrs. Turner. A swift punch of guilt slammed into her stomach, but it was instantly equipped by her realization of the amazing truth: Ludwig loved her and saw her as more than just the girl with whom he was carrying on an affair.

He kissed her forehead. "Please, darling, say something."

"Thank you, Ludwig." Tears of joy raced down Blanche's cheeks. "Oh, thank you, thank you."

"Don't worry about a thing." Ludwig drew her into his embrace. "Camellia will never know. I have sublet out a flat I lease just a few blocks away, a small place, but I can evict its tenants at once. You will be very comfortable there."

She was becoming a kept woman, Blanche realized with a strange little thrill of shock. If Mama had known... but Mama would never know. She'd left Blanche, just like everyone else in her life except for Ludwig, and if that meant being a kept woman, she would just have to be kept.

"Thank you," she said again. And she told herself, again, that everything would be all right. That none of this was that bad. That somehow Camellia's lack of love for Ludwig made it right for Blanche to be in love with him, to be sleeping with him. That her child would grow up with a loving father in a normal house and have a bright future.

She told herself all these things, even though, in her heart, she knew none of them were true.

***

MAY'S FACE, tiny as it was, was set in a mask of pure determination. The baby girl clutched the fabric of the sofa tightly in two chubby fists, her blonde curls bouncing over her shoulders as she strained to pull herself upright. Her baby socks – Blanche had knitted them herself – dug deep into the thick carpet, her tiny mouth working as she breathed heavily, hauling herself to her feet.

"That's it, baby," said Blanche, crouching on the floor a few feet away. The smell of baking pie and cinnamon flooded the flat from the kitchen's open door; it was snowing outside, but the crackle of the fire banished any cold from their cozy home.

"Come on," Blanche encouraged, holding out her arms. "I know you can do it this time, darling. Come on."

May studied her mother for a few moments with luminous eyes of forget-me-not blue. She lifted one hand from the sofa and held it out to Blanche, the little fingers outstretched.

"Yes. Yes, you can do it, May," Blanche said, clapping her hands and holding them out again. "Come on, darling, come on."

May let out a startling little giggle, a bubbling sound of pure joy that transfixed her face, her eyes dancing. Blanche felt everything melt inside her heart. Looking at this baby, she knew that there was nothing she wouldn't do for her. She would lay down her own life for this child. There was absolutely no question of it.

"Let go, darling," Blanche said. "Come on, May. You can do it."

Slowly, May's little fist lifted from the sofa, and she turned around with small, wobbling steps to face her mother. Holding out her small hands, her blue eyes fixed on Blanche, she took a tottering step forward.

Blanche's heart turned over in her chest with joy. Only a few feet of space separated them. "Again," she said, laughing. "Again, sweetie."

May chortled, the nervousness leaving her face. Arms held high, she stepped forward again, and again, and then came staggering over to Blanche in a rush with a squeal of glee, her small feet slapping on the carpet. She threw herself into her mother's arms, and Blanche caught her up tightly against her chest, hardly knowing if she was laughing or crying with joy.

"You did it," she cheered, smothering the baby with cuddles and kisses. "You walked, May. You walked all on your own."

There was a knock at the door, and Blanche straightened, shifting May onto her hip. Nervousness ran through her, as it always did. Had Camellia finally found them? But when she went to the window and twitched aside the curtains, there was a saddled horse tied in the street – the black one that Ludwig always rode when he came to visit.

"Papa's here," she told May, beaming.

May grinned widely, two lonely teeth wobbling in her smile. "Pap-pap-pap." she babbled. "Papapapapap."

"That's right." Blanche laughed, kissing her daughter's forehead. "Come on, let's go and say hello."

Ludwig was waiting on the threshold, holding a bouquet of flowers that filled the room with their jasmine scent. "Hello, my love," he said warmly, wrapping Blanche in a one-armed embrace and kissing her forehead.

"Come inside," said Blanche, tugging him into the flat by his coat and closing the door firmly behind him.

"Hello, little one." Ludwig tickled May's cheek, and the baby screeched and giggled.

"Pap-pap-pap," she yelled.

"Papa," said Ludwig. "Can you say that, darling? Papa."

"Pap-pap." laughed May.

"It'll come." Blanche smiled up at him, accepting his kiss. "How are you?"

"Ready for a slice of whatever you're baking," said Ludwig.

"Oh. The pie." Blanche thrust May into his arms. "It'll burn."

Ludwig scooped up the baby and Blanche hurried into the kitchen. In the doorway, she paused, glancing over her shoulder. Ludwig had the baby comfortably in the crook of his arm, and he was tickling her cheeks and crooning to her. She'd never known a man to love children so much, even his own.

If only he was her man, really, not one that she borrowed – or, rather, stole – from time to time. Yet every time she looked at him, was with him, she felt the weight of guilt growing heavier and heavier in her stomach.

CHAPTER 2

M<small>AY LAY STRETCHED</small> out on her belly, babbling quietly to herself as she stared at the rain trickling down the glass. She was a puny little thing on Blanche's broad, comfortable bed, a study of cuteness in pastel colours, her baby socks kicking this way and that as she propped herself up on her arms to stare at the raindrops trickling down the pane.

Blanche smiled despite the slowly growing worry that was creeping like a weed across her heart. "What do you see, baby?" she said.

May babbled nonsensically, her eyes fixed on the glittering raindrops. The soft patter of the rain on the roof only made the bedroom seemed warmer and cozier. Blanche's knitting needles clicked quietly as she tried to make another pair of socks. She'd had little luck with this knitting lark, apart from making a few rather lopsided blankets and some lumpy socks, but May didn't seem to mind if her socks were ugly. At least they were warm.

Knitting, and the fire crackling, and the sound of the rain, and May's tiny voice. Blanche tried to focus on these things and not on the fact that, for the first time since she could remember, Ludwig hadn't come to see her last week.

"Pap-pap," said May suddenly, slapping her chubby hands on the covers.

"Yes, darling," sighed Blanche. "I miss your papa, too."

"Pap-pap-pap-pap," squealed May and began to cry.

"May." Blanche set aside her knitting and quickly scooped the baby into her arms. "It's all right, dear. It's all right." She rocked the baby gently, wondering why these tears had come. May had just eaten and been changed; maybe she was tired. "Shhh. It's all right," Blanche murmured as May sobbed into her chest. "Time for a nap."

She walked over to the window, rocking May in her arms, and began to sing softly. "Hush, little baby, don't say a word. Papa's going to buy you a mockingbird..."

The notes of the lullaby fell as softly as the rain, and Blanche found herself holding back her tears. May didn't need a mockingbird, a diamond ring, a looking glass, a billy goat... She needed her father to visit, and, more practically, she needed the money he always brought. But Ludwig would come. Blanche had to be sure of it, or she would lose her mind. If he didn't come, what would become of them?

"And if that bull and cart fall down, you'll still be the sweetest little baby in town," Blanche sang.

May sighed, only half asleep, but at least she had stopped crying. Blanche turned to put her in her crib and heard a sudden, deep hammering on the door. She jumped, yanking May close to her chest again; the baby began to whimper at once.

More hammering. "Open up." A man's voice, one she didn't know.

Blanche stood frozen in the bedroom, clutching the squirming, whimpering baby. She was gripped with an overwhelming urge to run, but where to? There was only one door. She glanced swiftly at the window, but they were on the second floor. There was nothing to do except to creep over to the door, trembling when they knocked again.

"Open this door."

Blanche kept May clutched close to her in one arm and turned the knob just enough to open the door a crack. She peered through it, leaning her weight against it, half expecting something huge and evil to shove her aside and storm into her home.

"Who is it?" she quavered.

"It's your landlord, that's who it is," barked the man standing in the hallway. He was a short, stout creature with huge, hairy hands and small beady eyes that glittered with malice. Blanche had only seen him a few times before; Ludwig had always paid him in person, making sure of a generous tip to ensure the man's silence.

Blanche didn't know whether to feel relief or terror. Relief that this wasn't some stranger; terror because it had occurred to her, suddenly, that if Ludwig hadn't come this week, then the rent hadn't been paid.

She opened the door slowly, keeping May close. "How can I help you, sir?" she asked.

He gave her a contemptuous look, then swept past her into the flat, giving it a quick, disapproving glance. "You can get out of my flat, for a start."

"S-sir," Blanche stammered. It felt as though she'd been doused in cold water. "Sir, but – I – I live here – and my baby –"

"*Lived*. You *lived* here, Miss Eplett," said the landlord sternly. "The rent has not been paid, so I'm evicting you."

"Please, sir, you know that my – that Mr. Turner has the money," Blanche begged. May was crying loudly now. Blanche clung to the baby, trying to rock her, but her body seemed to have lost all sense of rhythm. "I know he hasn't been here in a little while, but I'm sure if you could speak with him…"

"Mr. Turner no longer has the money," said the landlord. He raised an eyebrow at her. "Did you expect that provision would be made for a mere harlot like you?"

Harlot. The word sank into her skin with unexpected brutality, but then again, Blanche realized, it was exactly the right word for her. It was exactly what she was. She thought she had come to terms with this in her heart but hearing the word like that from this angry little man suddenly made her realize it anew. It was so forceful that it took her a few seconds to register the rest of the sentence.

"I'm sorry," she said, "did you say – *provision*? What do you mean, provision?" Her voice trembled. "Mr. Turner has always provided for me." Her mind flew back to the last time he'd been here. He'd been laughing, playing with May, eating the dinner she made for him, infused with her desperate love. Had she said something wrong? Had he abandoned them?

Something changed in the landlord's face. He didn't relent, not quite, but his voice did lower a few octaves from an angry yell to something that was more like a mere snap.

"Don't you know about Mr. Turner?" he asked. "He's dead. So you and your disgusting ... child need to go."

Her stomach seemed to have been replaced with a small, cold stone.

She clutched the baby a little more closely.

May was more than that. And even if Blanche was the only person in the entire world who thought so, she would do whatever it took to make sure that the sins of May's parents would not be visited upon her.

PART II

CHAPTER 3

Six Years Later

BLANCHE QUIVERED WHERE SHE STOOD, trying her best to listen to Mrs. Watson's tirade through the terrible stabs of pain that were running through her belly. She wondered vaguely when the last time was she'd eaten. Two days ago? That seemed about right. Yesterday, she had had only tuppence left, and she'd bought some bread for May and done her best not to stare too intently while the child ate.

May. Blanche shivered on the doorstep, ignoring another gust of icy rain that was flung against her shrinking flesh. She needed to get back to her little girl.

"I'll fix it for you," Blanche mumbled, praying that Mrs. Watson wouldn't take away any of the pittance she was paying Blanche.

"You certainly will, and you won't charge me a ha'penny for it, do you understand?"

Blanche's heart skipped a beat. If Mrs. Watson took away anything, she wouldn't be able to pay both rent and food, and it would be the second day of hunger. "Of course, Mrs. Watson."

Somewhat appeased, the looming housekeeper let out a quiet snort. "Very well." She dug in the pocket of her greasy apron and produced a few small coins. "Here."

Blanche did her best not to snatch at the money. She clutched it gratefully, backing away. "Thank you very much, Mrs. – "

But the door had already been slammed in her face. The sound reminded her of what it had been like that very first year, as she wandered from house to house, begging for work as a scullery-maid with her baby bundled in rags on her hip. They had slept in alleyways under bits of newspaper. May had grown sick once, so sick that Blanche feared she would lose the only thing she had left to love, but somehow, she had survived. But none of that was thanks to any of the people in the rich houses like the one Ludwig had had. All of them had taken just one glance at the baby on Blanche's hip and slammed the door in her face, no matter how she protested that she'd find someone to care for May, that the little girl would be no trouble at all.

Where's the child's father? so many people had demanded. When Blanche said he was dead, that she was nothing but a poor widow, they had glared at her bare left ring finger – devoid of even the twist of iron that the poorest women wore – and slammed the door nonetheless.

She clutched the bundle of torn clothes tightly to her chest, taking a few deep breaths to dispel the memories. Things were better now. At least they had a tenement, even if it was a pitiful one, and she had enough money to pay for it and for a few scraps of food and even a little coal on the coldest winter days. It was all thanks to the little bit of mending she'd been able to do for Mrs. Watson and her other friends on this street: middle-class women with big, rambunctious families who often tore their clothes but didn't quite have the money to buy new ones each time. Harsh though they were, at least they'd given Blanche a chance.

And, more crucially, they'd given May a chance to survive.

Blanche dug her fingers into the bundle as she walked, her teeth gritting. That was the goal. That was all she needed. A chance for May to survive.

THE HOUSE WAS huge and scary. Not that the piece of the house that belonged to May and Mama was huge at all. It was tiny, actually, a little section of some old room roped off with a piece of curtain. There was just enough space for the sleeping pallet, and the tiny fireplace, and the trunk that held everything they owned.

And the sewing table.

May swung her legs as she sat on the upturned bucket Mama used as a stool, humming to herself as she studied the fabric in front of her in the faint light from the single, tiny, grimy window above her head. She had to hum, otherwise the sounds of the house around her would grow too loud, and they were such scary sounds. Whoops and yells. Awful, hacking coughs. The wind moaning in the holes in the walls, even though Mama had stuffed old newspapers into those holes. The wind still found its way in, singing its mournful song in the holes, poking its freezing fingers down the back of May's shirt and into her ears.

The worst sound was the crying, of course. Somewhere in this vast old building, someone's baby was always crying and crying and crying. They all had such small, reedy voices. May hated the crying, but she hated it even more when she could hear it getting weaker and weaker.

Until it eventually stopped.

She tried not to think about the crying babies. She tried not to think about the cold that was nibbling at her blue fingers or of how hungry she was. Instead, she looked at the scraps of fabric on the big wooden box that Mama used as a sewing desk, then slowly lifted the needle that Mama kept so carefully in a matchbox. It was very sharp — she had learned this the hard way — but it was also capable of a kind of magic. She had taken half an hour to thread it, but it was done at last, and now she could begin to sew.

May held up the two little scraps. One was pale blue; the other, faded white. Both were smaller than her palm, but she thought that they looked like the sky and a cloud next to each other. If she folded the white one in half, it was small enough to look like a little cloud. She'd seen clouds before, out of the tenement window. Sometimes she'd even seen clouds outside, but Mama didn't like to let her go outside.

She folded up the white one, laid it over the blue, then moved it this way and that until it was just so — just the way she wanted it. Carefully, she started to sew, tucking the needle through the two rags in a row of stitches around the edge of the white one. A few times, the needle jabbed painfully into her finger. She cried a little then, and sucked at her fingers, and sat in the corner humming to herself and trying not to hear the terrible fight Mr. and Mrs. Higgs were having on the other side of the curtain. But each time the rags called her back, and she got up and went back to work on them.

She was just trying to tie off the last stitch when she heard Mama's cheerful voice greeting the Higgs, then the crinkle of the curtain that formed one wall of their tiny, triangular tenement. Looking up, she froze at first, but immediately relaxed when she saw Mama's dear face as she ducked past the curtain.

"Mama, Mama." She set down the needle and jumped from the bucket, holding up her masterpiece. "Look what I made."

Mama set down the bundle of clothes she'd brought back to be fixed. "What is this?"

"There were some rags lying on the box, so I made this," said May proudly. "Look – it's a blue sky with a little cloud."

Mama was turning the rags over in her hands, this way and that, and May felt a flutter of nervousness in her stomach. Mama was very seldom angry, but when she was, it was on days like this: days when her eyes were so very red, her skin so very pale, and the circles under her eyes so very deep and black.

But when Mama looked up at May, her eyes were wide. "Did you make these stitches?" she asked. "All on your own?"

May straightened, pride filling her. "Yes, Mama, I did."

"Show me." Mama set the rags down on the box.

May scrambled up onto the stool. "I need a piece of green, Mama," she said. "To make grass."

Mama found a scrap of yellow somewhere, and May was sad about this at first, but then Mama explained that the yellow could be a beach. Excited, May took it from her, retrieved the needle and thread, and slowly began to make a row of stitches to attach the beach to the sky. Mama leaned over her, holding her breath the whole way.

"There." May set down the needle, grinning up at Mama. The look of surprise and joy on Mama's face was the most wonderful thing May had seen in a long time. "Is it pretty, Mama?"

"Oh, May, darling, it's beautiful," said Mama, lifting up her little composition of three rags. "I love it." Her eyes were bright in a way May hadn't seen for ages.

"You can have it," May said. She would have given away anything, her left arm, her eyes, for Mama to always have that look on her face and not the deep, brooding frown that was normally there. "It's yours."

"Oh, sweetie." Mama kissed the side of May's head, cuddling her with one arm. "I think we'll put it up on the wall, and then it can be both of ours." She paused. "Do you like sewing things?"

"I like it very much, Mama. Sometimes I prick my fingers, though."

"I can find you a thimble. I know I can." Mama paused. "Would you like to sew some more, May? Some patches, like Mama does?"

"Can't I sew more pretty things?" May asked.

"Maybe, when we have extra rags again." Mama touched her cheek. "But what about some patches? I'll help you."

"All right." May grinned. It would be better than sitting alone in a corner while Mama worked by candlelight, shushing her harshly anytime her play really started to be any fun at all. "I want to try."

"That's my baby girl." Mama turned to the bundle, and her hands were shaking just a little.

May hoped they were shaking from excitement and not weakness. These days, it was hard to tell.

※

Taylor Harris' throat was hurting again. He hoped it didn't mean anything this time, although in Taylor's experience, his throat hurting was never a good thing.

He walked quickly along the street, dodging the muddier bits of pavement with his bare toes as he kept his hands pressed firmly into the tattered pockets of his threadbare coat. The wind was brutal this morning, finding its way between the chinks of his clothes and through all of the little holes that were starting to appear in his shirt, nipping at his bare ribs and shrunken belly. He huddled deeper into his coat, quickened his pace despite the ache of hunger and exhaustion that sucked at his limbs.

It was when his throat began to hurt that things had really gone wrong with the Hunters. He had been filled with so much hope when they'd come to the orphanage to adopt him, even when they'd taken him home and put him to work in their cotton mill. The mill hadn't been nice, but at least he'd had three meals a day, even if he'd had to crawl underneath the rattling, snapping, booming cotton mule with its vicious teeth and spinning parts to get the bits of dust and lint out from under it. The air had been thick with dust, but at least it had been warm, even if it had made him cough. Even if it had made his throat hurt.

Even if it had finally made him too sick to work. Too sick to be useful. That was the day that Mr. Hunter had pushed him out onto the street and slammed the mill's door in his face, and he had realized he was truly on his own.

A hansom-cab sped toward him, toward the big icy puddle in the street in the path of its wheels, and Taylor skipped quickly to the side to avoid the sheet of cold water the cab spat into the air. He ducked under the arm of the policeman directing traffic, then disappeared into the crowd before the bobby even knew he'd been there.

Across the street, following the tide of a bunch of little boys off to school—plump, well-groomed little boys, pushing and shoving and laughing with one another. Taylor wondered where they found the energy. He left them behind, slipped down an alley, clambered onto an upturned barrel and scrambled onto the top of a narrow wall, one brick wide.

The wall had spikes on the top, but they were narrow, and Taylor had tiny, undernourished feet. He balanced expertly on the balls of his feet, gripping the wall on the other side of the tall iron, his thin wrists fitting easily between the spikes. They weren't all that sharp, truth be told, although they'd make the wall hard to climb if you weren't a thin, agile ten-year-old boy.

He peered down into the courtyard below. It was small, and contained mostly just a few rubbish bins, and a sack off to one side that immediately caught his eye.

There was no use searching the bins, Taylor knew. The workhouse didn't throw any food away. He could hardly comprehend how anyone could throw food away, so it did not surprise him that workhouse inmates ate vegetables with the peels on and cores with the apple and sucked bones so clean that they looked like they'd been boiled. But that sack – that was what held the real treasures.

He slipped down the other side of the wall, a quick, easy movement, and scampered over to the sack. Already, he could hear a loud voice coming down the hall toward this scruffy little back door to the tall, austere building. The men burned these clothes – which were removed from new intakes – every morning. He was just in time. Grabbing the sack, he opened it, glanced quickly inside to confirm that it contained some rags, and then grabbed a rubbish bin, dragging it over to the wall.

The workhouse door slammed open. "Hey!" yelled a voice.

Taylor scrambled onto the bin and up the wall in one movement as running feet pounded into the courtyard. Long before anyone could think to follow, he was over the wall and down the street, the bag of rags bouncing on his back.

He couldn't jog for long. Just long enough that the shouting faded into the distance. Slowing back to a walk, Taylor stumbled, halted, leaned against the wall of a cobbler's shop and struggled to take deep breaths without coughing. At least the wind was good for something; when he turned into it, it made it a little easier to breathe, even though it seemed filled with tiny knives of cold that cut through his lungs.

He went on his way walking briskly, the bag over his shoulder, his free hand still in his pocket to protect his bare fingers from the cold. A few minutes later, his bare feet had left the muddy pavement behind for pure mud that sucked at his freezing toes. He dodged it as well as he could, picking his way carefully between buildings that towered in claustrophobic closeness on either side of him, sheer brick walls glaring grimly down with no adornment to soften their harsh surfaces. Most of the windows were boarded up; those that weren't had tatty curtains floating out of them, driven by the breeze, holey and yellowed.

Taylor's chest was just beginning to tighten once more when he stepped out from between two of those eerie buildings and called out, "Good mornin', Old Rags."

The dour old rag-and-bone man was busy harnessing his donkey to a ramshackle old cart, itself constructed from little more than old planks and ragged blankets. The donkey's hips jutted north and south like a hat stand, and its ears drooped sideways as it sagged in its makeshift harness, cobbled together from old ropes. Old Rags looked up at the sound of Taylor's voice, his face twisted and wizened by years of suffering. Taylor wondered if his own face would look like this, with time.

"I've got some good ones for you, guv," he said, holding up the bag and then dropping it triumphantly at Old Rags' feet.

The old man poked around in the bag, grunting. Taylor waited patiently. The donkey slept. Finally, Old Rags straightened, patted his pockets and grunted unintelligibly. He withdrew a sixpence and held it out to Taylor in a withered, bony hand, trembling with weakness and draped in rags.

"Thank'ee, guv," said Taylor, taking it gratefully.

Old Rags swatted at the air between them and stumbled back to the donkey. Taylor watched him go, wondering if he had also been a little boy one day, a long time ago. A little boy with a name, before he became Old Rags.

And he wondered if he, too, would one days lose everything about himself except the fact that he sold bits of rubbish on the street.

MAMA WAS PLEADING with Mr. Higgs again. It seemed that pleading with Mr. Higgs had to happen every Sunday night, when they were sorting out the money they had to give to the landlord when he came every Monday morning. May didn't like the landlord; he was a snooty person, with very shiny shoes, who always stepped delicately around the ominously dark spots on the floor of the tenement rooms.

But she liked Mr. Higgs even less than she liked the landlord. His voice was loud and raspy, and he was always, always smoking. Mama always said that Mr. Higgs' smoking was the reason why the family had to live in a tiny, ugly tenement like this one, even though Mr. and Mrs. Higgs both had work and three of the children worked, too. Everyone except Freddy, who couldn't walk and just sat in a corner most of the time, crying a little. May hated to listen to him cry.

He was crying now, while she heard Mr. and Mrs. Higgs' strident voices arguing with Mama about the money. Her heart stung to listen to him. Poor Freddy. He was only a little bit older than she was, and his life was so, so lonely. Sometimes Mrs. Higgs would scream at him, and he would cry even more.

She hummed to herself, but the humming couldn't drown out the Higgs' voices, so she went over to her little sewing station. Her fingers were sore from sewing all week to help Mama, but she had ended up with a little pile of scraps, and she was so excited to see what she could make with them. Clambering up onto the makeshift stool, May began to work.

It took her a few minutes to make those bits of rags into the picture she'd drawn in her mind the moment she'd seen them all lying there together, her reward for a week of hard work. The big rag was a bit more torn than she'd anticipated, but she managed to cobble together the edge just enough to be able to fold it around most of the smaller rags, making a nice round bubble. That left her with two more little rags. She cut them carefully into half-moons with Mama's precious scissors and sewed them onto the top of the stuffed round ball. Finally, she picked up a bit of charcoal from the fire and drew something like a face, with big eyes, a smiley mouth and six straight lines for whiskers.

Holding her creation, she sneaked over to the curtain separating their tenement from the Higgs'. Peering through one of the curtain's many holes, she saw that Mama and the Higgses were standing in the furthest corner; Mama was furious, waving her arms, and Mr. Higgs was jabbing an angry finger at her. Her eyes darted to the opposite corner, where Freddy was sitting, his hands over his face, sobbing.

The sight gave May just enough courage to slip underneath the curtain and scamper over to him, clutching the little creature she'd made. She stopped a few feet away from him.

"Freddy?" she whispered.

The child raised his face from his hands slowly. He sat with his back up against the walls, his stick-thin legs stuck out on the floor. It was no wonder he couldn't walk, May thought.

She didn't think she'd be able to walk either if her legs were so very thin. They were like little matchsticks stretched out in front of him.

Her heart stung for him now as his father's shouting echoed around the room. His pallid cheeks glimmered with tears. She'd heard his mother slapping him, and she realized that this tiny, reeking tenement was Freddy's entire world. He didn't even have a window to peer out of or feet to carry him across the room for a new perspective.

He was watching her a little fearfully now. She crept nearer, doing her best to avoid Mr. Higgs' attention.

"Hello," she whispered.

Freddy's eyes flickered with fear. "Hello," he hazarded.

"I made you something." May stretched out an arm, her creation resting in the palm of her hand.

Freddy shuffled a little closer, wincing as he did so. She wondered if he could feel his thin seat bones pressing against the harsh floor. A dreadful reek emanated from around him when he moved, and May held her breath, trying her best to pretend she hadn't noticed.

"What is it?" he asked, reaching out a hand, then drawing it back again as if thinking better of it.

"It's a cat," said May. "A friendly cat. Look, it's smiling."

Freddy studied it for a few moments. "Its ears are a bit round."

May gave it a critical look. "You're right. Its ears are *much* too round. I'll cut them."

"No – please don't." Freddy reached out, snatching it from her hand almost reflexively, like he hadn't really meant to grab it. "I... I like it."

He gave her something that flickered on his face rather like a smile, drawing back thin lips from teeth that looked too big for his mouth, if only for a moment. Then he tucked the little creature closer to his chest, cradling it like something unspeakably precious.

"Thank you," he whispered, tears filling his eyes.

Mr. Higgs' voice rose then, and May's courage failed her, although she wasn't sure what she feared the most: Freddy's tears, or his father's wrath. She turned and scampered back behind the curtain, then curled up on the pallet, pulling their thin blanket over her head.

She would make more of these, she decided. She would make sure every Freddy in this tenement had something small and soft that they liked.

Something all their own.

BLANCHE COULDN'T BELIEVE May was still at the sewing table when she came home from taking the latest batch of mending to Mrs. Watson. She stood looking through the curtain for a few moments, watching her child where she bent over the makeshift table, her quick little fingers dancing in the dim light of a candle stub, the needle flashing as she worked. May was only eight years old. Still so very little. Yet the delicate little frown on her face was the look of an expert hard at work.

And she *was* an expert, Blanche realized. Mrs. Watson hadn't complained about the mending in a long, long time. In fact, she had begun to notice an extra penny or two being slipped into her hand. May's work was lasting, and some days, Mrs. Watson even gave her a look of something like respect.

In Blanche's life, respect was even harder to come by than money or food.

But May wasn't busy with mending now. She was making something else: a tiny animal, stuffed with the off-cuts they couldn't make into patches, using the little bits of fabric that Blanche could spare (or couldn't really spare, but she did beg so prettily). Her bright blue eyes were sparkling with interest as she tied off a last stitch, laid the needle aside and raised the tiny object to the light. Blanche could just about see the shape of a tiny head, with flaps for ears and a bit of string for a tail. It looked like a little dog.

She smiled, basking in the unrelenting love for this child who had been the only spark in her heart for so many years now. May was everything to her. She felt terrible about the poor child doing all the mending, but at moments like this, Blanche realized that May truly did love sewing. It made her feel a little better.

And it gave her hope that May might have the one thing that had never been on the cards for Blanche: a better future.

Brushing the curtain aside, she slipped into the room. "Hello, darling."

May looked up at her, her eyes brightening. She set down her creation and ran to Blanche, throwing her arms around her mother's waist. "Mama. You're back."

Her joyous little voice rang around the miserable tenement, drowning out the hollow whimper of the wind in the holey walls and the distant cries of some starving baby. Blanche leaned down, hugging May, kissing her golden head. "I love you."

"I love you, Mama." May stepped back. "Look what I'm making."

Blanche admired the little object as May held it up to show her. The child's sewing had improved at a frightening pace, even though it had been just three months since May had started doing the mending. The little dog had a neatly sewn head with a jutting muzzle and a slender neck leading down into the plump, round body.

"He's a rather fat little dog," said Blanche.

May giggled, delighted. "I just need to work out how to make legs." She picked up a bit of charcoal, sitting back down at the makeshift desk, and carefully drew the dog a few paws on the bottom. "Then I can make animals standing up, not just lying down."

"I'm sure you'll work it out," said Blanche, meaning every word. May seemed to have an incredible aptitude for seeing pictures in her mind, and then using fabrics to bring them to life.

May held up the dog. "What do you think?"

Blanche took it from her, turning it this way and that. She thought it was attractive, and cheaply made, and that there were people out there with more money than she had but not quite enough money to buy toys from the toymaker... and that perhaps they could be persuaded to buy these for a few desperately needed extra pennies.

"It's lovely," she said, then, choosing her words carefully, "May, darling, what would you think if we sold it, and bought some extra food?"

May's face fell at once. "Are you hungry, Mama?"

Blanche had been hungry since they'd been thrown out of the Turner flat. But she couldn't tell May that. "I think *you're* hungry, darling," she said, trying to keep her desperation from showing on her face.

"I made him for little Reggie Fields down the hall," May said quietly. "They had a dog before his papa died, and he misses him so much."

Tears were hovering in her eyes, and Blanche felt another swift pang of guilt. She was already making her child do most of her work. Could she really deny her the genuine kindness that filled her heart?

"Then you must give him to Reggie," Blanche decided. She rested a hand on May's head. "But do you think you could make some more of these, some extra ones, to sell? Perhaps they would bring joy to other children."

May considered this for a moment, looking up at Blanche. "Could we have something to eat twice a day then, Mama?"

"Maybe," said Blanche, not wanting to make extravagant promises.

May smiled. "I think I could do that," she said solemnly. "But I still want to give everyone in the whole tenement one of these."

How had this perfect creature come into this fallen world?

"That's very sweet of you, my dear," she said, gathering May in her arms and kissing her soft little cheek. "You're a kind heart, May. Never change. Always be this way."

May snuggled against Blanche's chest. "Yes, Mama."

It was good she didn't know, Blanche thought, how easily kindness could fall away in the face of desperation. It was good May didn't know how easy it was to fall into a black hole of wrongdoing that one would never be able to get away from.

It was good May didn't know she'd been born of Blanche's wrongdoing, and that Blanche would feel guilty every day for the rest of her life because of the fact that her failure had resulted in the most wonderful gift she could ever have asked for.

CHAPTER 4

The city was so big.

May didn't get to walk outside very much, so on this day, she was making sure to take in everything she saw, her wide eyes searching every detail of the world around her. It was only a very short way to the market to buy soup, and May had walked this path many times before. But every time was an adventure compared to the tenement.

Today was beautiful: the breeze was crisp, but for once, warm, bright sunshine was pouring profusely down over the streets, shimmering on the puddles that lay in the many potholes, glancing off the grimy surfaces of windows that were almost never cleaned. Tipping back her chin to look up past the towering brick walls around her, May peered through the smog overhead, catching a glimpse of a brilliantly blue sky.

All around her, the city trundled on in its muted tones: its grays and browns, its blacks and grubby whites. But above her, the sky was like a glorious slice of pure colour. She wondered what it would be like to reach up and grasp hold of that colour, and pull it down hand over hand, and wrap it around her body. She could accentuate it with raindrops that would sparkle diamond-bright at her waist and in long bright trails down her skirt. She could decorate it with cloud-like lace at her throat and wrists. A deep sigh escaped her, the wonderful daydream spinning in her mind, pure beauty.

Keeping the money clutched tightly in her fist, she looked back down at the streets, slightly dizzy from staring up at the sky. Right now, pure beauty was going to be a bowl of hot soup from the toothless street vendor at the corner of the market. Mama was off taking the mending to Mrs. Watson; she'd be back soon, with enough money for their portion of the rent and then some, so May could buy soup with no problem.

Squelching down to the end of the street, May peered cautiously out at the crossroads in front of her. It was busier here. People were moving this way and that; here and there someone had a donkey cart plodding miserably along the pavement, but most of the traffic was on foot, a faceless hustle of ragged figures. Mama had always told May to stay away from crowds of people in case there were naughty boys there who would pick your pockets. She had her money clenched in her fist, of course, but the sight of the crowd filled her with nervousness. She'd seldom seen so many people in one place before.

Her eyes darted to the left. There was an alley between buildings here. If she followed it, perhaps it would take her to the other side of the street, albeit in something of a roundabout way. She'd never gone this way before, but the thought sent a tingle of excitement through her. It was better to go to a new place than walk among so many people.

She turned and moved down the alley, slowly, stepping carefully to avoid the broken bottles, bits of glass, dead rats and old bones littering the mud. Humming to herself, she kept her fist clenched over the money. There was a gentle curve in the alley, and when she rounded it, she found herself brought up short against a brick wall with tall, iron spikes against the top. To her right stood an iron gate, also topped with spikes. It was open just a crack.

Disappointed, May was about to turn away. Clearly this alleyway led nowhere. Then she heard two voices behind the wall: both women, one nasal, one gruff.

"Ugh. Did you see the girl who came in wearing these? She was dreadful," complained the gruff voice. "Red all over where she'd been scratching herself."

The nasal voice had an audible shudder in it. "Poor girl. At least she'll be spared *that* now she's here."

"That and not much else, poor mite." The gruff voice had a note of empathy in it. "I don't give her more than a week."

What appalling place was this where people came to die? May stared up at it, frightened, realizing that this was much bigger even than the tenement building where she lived. There were tiny, narrow windows, like arrow slits, and it towered four brick stories above her head. A grim pall hung about the place, as though it was wreathed in shadow despite the sunshine glowing on its bricks.

She began to back away, but the word *clothes* caught her attention, and she stopped.

"... burning their old clothes," the nasal voice was saying. "Seems a bit harsh."

"Well, there's a good reason for it," said the gruff voice. "And in any case, I'm telling you, that girl doesn't have any need of these anymore."

"I suppose not." The nasal voice paused. "Should I run and close the gate?"

"No," said the gruff voice dismissively. "Gregory left it open, and he can shut it. He'll be back soon. Besides, no one wants these sorry old rags."

Rags. May turned around, her heart hammering with possibilities. Rags. *She* wanted rags. The more rags she had, the more little animals she could make and give to the tenement children – or give to Mama to sell on the streets, so that they could eat soup more often. Maybe every day.

She waited until she heard the *thunk* of a slamming door and then edged forward, her heart pounding in her mouth. Slowly, she pushed the iron gate aside and peered into what seemed to be a narrow courtyard surrounded by those high walls. There were a few bins here, all of them empty right now, and over there, in the corner, a bundle of ragged clothes lying against the wall.

May's eyes almost popped out of her head. There was a whole armload of rags there. And she'd just heard those women say no one wanted them. Surely, then, she could take them. No one would miss them. No one would even know.

Thrusting the money into the front of her dress, she scampered forward, careful not to disturb a thing. Her skin crawled under the frown of the huge building where it glowered at her. She bent down, grabbed the rags, and tucked them all close to her chest.

Then she turned and bolted, her prize held firmly in her arms, straight back home to show Mama.

BLANCHE CLOSED HER EYES, letting out a long sigh of delight as the warm soup slid down into her stomach. When she looked down into her bowl, the mixture was watery, and not even hot enough to steam much in this cold room; but there were real vegetables floating in it, and she thought she'd even spotted a few scraps of meat and bones as well. Whatever was in this mystery soup, it was so good to eat something hot and at least a little wholesome.

She smiled over at May, who was perched on the upside-down bucket, kicking her legs impatiently as she ate her soup. The little girl's eyes were distant. She wasn't looking at the row of tiny stuffed animals she'd set out on the sewing desk, completed and ready for sale. Blanche, on the other hand, couldn't take her eyes off them. They were all so sweet: little foxes and donkeys, a bunch of birds, mice with long tails made of thread twisted together. Blanche's personal favorite was the wolf, which had rather scary teeth that May had drawn on with charcoal.

"For little boys, Mama," May had said seriously. "Freddy told me that other little boys like scary things."

Blanche was glad that May was spending a little time with a child near her own age. Her only fear was that poor Freddy wouldn't live very long and would soon break May's heart. But how could she tell her child that? Being a mother, she thought, must be the most impossible thing in the world. And yet she had no idea how she would have survived without this impossibility.

Right now, May was looking at the pile of rags beside the sewing desk where she'd put them yesterday after bringing them home from the streets somewhere. She'd been so excited about those rags that she'd quite forgotten about the soup, and Blanche had had to go out and buy some. May had been overwhelmed with joy to have enough materials to work with, even if those rags had been the smelliest, dirtiest things that Blanche had seen in a long time before she'd soaked and washed them in cold water. She could only hope May hadn't taken them from the workhouse nearby. It was impossible to tell – May hadn't exactly been able to explain where she'd found them – but they would certainly make plenty of stuffed animals. And the stuffed animals were rapidly becoming their most important source of income.

"What are you thinking of, darling?" Blanche asked softly.

May took another mouthful of soup, almost without noticing it. "What has shorter legs, Mama?" she asked. "A rabbit, or a badger?"

Blanche wasn't certain. She only knew what a badger was because she'd seen one at the bottom of the Turners' garden a lifetime ago. "I think a badger, probably. Why?"

"I think badger legs will be easier to make," said May. "I'm going to make a badger with legs tonight."

Blanche smiled. "Aren't you tired of making things, darling?"

"No, not one bit." May grinned. "I want to make a badger. With legs."

Before Blanche could respond, a sudden howl rose from the tenement beside them, lancing easily through the curtain. It was Mr. Higgs.

"MISS EPLETT," he was roaring, and there was a thundering of heavy boots on the floor as he approached the curtain.

Blanche felt her blood turn to ice. She scrambled to her feet, rushing to the curtain before Mr. Higgs could burst inside and frighten poor May.

"What is it, Mr. Higgs?" she asked, pulling the curtain aside.

He was standing mere inches from her, his hands curled into meaty fists.

"I know it was you," he snarled. "I know it."

"What?" Blanche said.

"You did this." Mr. Higgs grasped one greasy sleeve and yanked it back, revealing a blue-veined arm pock-marked with tiny, red flecks. It looked like any other nasty, unwashed arm to Blanche, who stared at him. "Did what?"

"You brought lice into this tenement," Mr. Higgs thundered.

Blanche's heart faltered within her. She looked more closely. The red flecks were tiny, unmistakable bite marks, and when she leaned closer, she could see that the spots on Mr. Higgs' skin were more than just dirt. They were squirming and crawling and burrowing.

Repulsed, she drew back, and Mr. Higgs let out a triumphant snort. "I saw those dreadful, ratty rags your child brought back yesterday," he barked. "Smelled them, too. And now look at this. Don't you know that I have enough troubles without this?"

May. Blanche whirled around, looking back through the curtain. May had pushed her soup aside; she was turning a rag this way and that, and Blanche knew that she was planning how she was going to turn it into a badger. As Blanche watched, the little girl reached up absently and scratched her arm, and she could already see the little red marks rising on them.

So she *had* taken those rags from the workhouse.

She turned back to the furious tenant. "Mr. Higgs, I – "

"I don't want to hear it." Mr. Higgs yanked his sleeve back down over his arm. "I want you out of this tenement."

Blanche's stomach plummeted with horror at those words. Where could she go? She had fought tooth and nail just to secure this tenement.

"Please, Mr. Higgs – " she began again.

"I have no interest in your pleading, woman," Mr. Higgs trumpeted, pointing imperiously to the door. "I want you out. Take your illegitimate, lousy brat and leave at once."

Something began to boil in the pit of Blanche's stomach. That same fire that had been keeping her alive, that had been feeding her every action since May was just a tiny girl, began to roar and leap and flare within her.

"I think not, Mr. Higgs," she roared.

Mr. Higgs took a step back, shocked that some unmarried wench like her would raise her voice to him. It was that shock that gave her the only advantage she was likely to get.

She clenched her fists, taking an aggressive step nearer. "I sourced this tenement and welcomed you and your family into it. The landlord knows *me* – especially since you insist on sending me to pay him every time. I am not going anywhere, and neither is my beautiful daughter."

Mr. Higgs was still pale, but his lip curled in a snarl at her words. Still, they both knew she was right.

"Well, then, I suppose we'll be the ones to leave," he hissed. Globbing up a gout of filthy saliva, he spat it at her feet. It took all of her strength not to jump back in horror at the sight. "There are plenty of desperate people with space in their tenements in this city." Mr. Higgs delivered his parting shot in a snarl of rage, then whirled around and strode away, leaving Blanche trembling with exhaustion and fear.

The rent was all hers to pay now.

And even though there was no door, just the soft curtain falling back over the space, Blanche could still hear a slamming shut in the depths of her soul.

Blanche's pockets were conspicuously empty as she gazed down into their single, large, cast-iron pot balanced over the little fireplace. Her last coins had gone to buying all the coal she could afford, and even so, half the coal was gone and the water in the pot had barely reached a boil. She stirred at it with a stick she'd taken from the park on the way home from the market. Nameless filth and the countless corpses of tiny lice clung to the stick; the same water had been used to give herself and May a rudimentary wash in a bid to rid themselves of those lice.

"Is it ready yet, Mama?" May asked.

Blanche looked over at her. She'd almost forgotten how pretty her little daughter was when she was clean. Her soft golden curls spilled over her shoulders in shining ringlets; when she raised her face to Blanche's, her skin was rosy pink. Somehow, Blanche had managed to raise a beautiful, healthy daughter in this disgusting place.

So far.

"It's ready," said Blanche. "Stay back."

She used the stick and the tips of her fingers to lift the sack in which she'd put all the lousy rags and the equally lousy stuffed animals, tipping them all into the boiling water. Spluttering and hissing, the filthy water enveloped the rags and May's little creations.

"Stir gently, Mama," said May nervously. "I don't want the stitches to pull apart."

Blanche gritted her teeth as a terrible stench rose from the boiling water. She thought she'd washed the poverty from the workhouse rags in cold water last night, but apparently it was almost part of their fabric. She shuddered at the sight of the dead lice floating to the top of the dreadful, bubbling mixture. The nauseating smell filled every corner of their tenement.

And the empty tenement next door.

The Higgses were conspicuously absent. It was strange not to hear Mr. Higgs' grumbling voice or Freddy's occasional pipe from behind the curtain, and May kept glancing over her shoulder, wondering where he'd gone.

"Where did Freddy go?" May asked softly.

Blanche glanced at her, then turned back to her work. "They moved away, my love."

"But where?"

"I... don't know." Blanche paused. "Somewhere nicer, I think."

"Oh." May's little face relaxed into a smile. "That's good. Freddy didn't like it here."

But you're stuck here. Blanche scratched absently at another bite mark on the inside of her left elbow, worrying that poor May would be lonely, worrying again that this would make her work less productively, and then feeling deeply guilty for thinking of that. But there was only one way they would make enough money for the full rent now: they had to sell as many stuffed animals as they could.

After a few minutes, the fire began to sputter as the coals grew spent, and the surface of the water was thick with a carpet of dead lice.

"There," said Blanche, forcing a cheerfulness she couldn't feel. "I think they'll be all clean now."

May hurried eagerly to her side as she began to ladle the rags out of the disgusting pot and into a large tin bowl on top of the sewing desk.

"Keep your hands behind your back, darling. I don't want you to touch these yet - they're very hot," Blanche cautioned. Again, the worry that May might burn a hand. Again, the worry that that would keep her from working. Again, the terrible guilt. Blanche didn't know if she'd ever be able to repay the world for all the sins she had committed.

"Oh," May cried out, dismayed.

Blanche sucked in a breath, withdrawing the ladle, recognizing at once the pattern of brown and faded blue of the damp rag she'd just laid in the bowl. It was surrounded by tiny, squashed balls of other small bits of rag, and with tatters of thread.

"My badger," May breathed, her eyes filling with tears. She reached out a hand as though to touch it, then drew it back. "Oh, my badger is all ruined."

"May, my dear, I'm so sorry," said Blanche.

May raised her face to Blanche's, heartbreak written in the depths of her blue eyes, and mustered a wobbling smile. "I'll make him again," she whimpered, wiping at her tears. "Better, this time."

"I'll help you," said Blanche.

What else was there to say to those soft and courageous blue eyes, even if her hands ached from the stirring, and her head ached from the smell, and her heart ached from the weight of it all? She couldn't give up. Not so long as May kept trying.

CHAPTER 5

The little girl dragged again at her father's sleeve. "Papa, Papa, look."

Her father was hunched and shuffling with exhaustion, his eyes staring. While his shoes looked warm and sturdy compared to May's bare feet where they shrank upon the pavement, they were scuffed and worn, and his jacket had been mended many times already. He tugged his sleeve away. "Come on, poppet. We need to go home."

"Oh, but Papa, they're so beautiful," breathed the little girl, her eyes very wide and very bright against the grey street. She had shoes too; they looked far newer than her father's, and her hair was neatly washed and braided, as though she was coming home from school. "Look – they're such lovely toys."

"We can't have toys right now, pet," sighed her father, and the sigh seemed to come from somewhere deep and hopeless within him.

"Tuppence each, sir," cried May. She crouched down to where the little toys were lined up on the pavement in front of her, selecting a bird with long, trailing tail feathers made of strips of rag. "Only tuppence." She held up the bird, trailing it this way and that through the air so that its rag feathers fanned out.

"Oh," gasped the little girl, coming to a dead stop.

Her father was forced to look up. His eyes dwelled on May for a moment, softening, and then he turned his attention to the bird. "Well, then," he said, very quietly. "That is rather something."

"I love it," breathed the little girl, her eyes fixed on the bird.

May loved the expression in her eyes, loved the sheer wonder she saw there. It was hard to find wonder in this world with its towering walls and grimy air. But there was wonder high above them, in that slice of blue sky she saw from time to time, and she had tried to put all that wonder into the little bird until it was as much a part of the tiny object as its stitches and stuffing.

"Tuppence, you say?" said the father.

The little girl turned pleading eyes on him. "Oh, *please*, Papa."

"You have been a very good little girl at school lately," her father murmured. He dug in his pocket, producing a tuppence. "Does your mother make these?"

"No, sir," said May, enunciating *sir* just like Mama taught her. "I do."

"Well, you have a dab hand at sewing, little one." The father dropped the tuppence in her hand. "There you are, pet."

"Oh, thank you, Papa, thank you, thank you," gasped the little girl, taking the bird and running a circle on the pavement with it so that its feathers flared in the wind.

No one paused to thank May, but she didn't mind; the look of joy on the girl's face, and the look of love on her father's, were all she needed.

As they walked away, she heard the distant chimes as Big Ben sonorously announced a quarter to four. Mama wanted her back home by half past four at the latest, so she had to get going. Besides, she had some good ideas for new toys when she got there.

Gathering up the two or three toys that hadn't been sold, she tucked them into her pockets with the money that people had given her and started to skip along the pavement, humming. *Row, row, row your boat, gently down the stream.* It was a good rhythm to skip to, and the streets were still quite empty; she could take nice, big skips. She wondered briefly if she should go back to the marketplace and buy some soup. But Mama had seemed worried when Mr. Higgs had left. They'd just have bread again tonight, she supposed.

All she needed now was more rags to make her toys with. She skipped down the alleyway, quieting her hum, and paused beneath the tall wall with its spikes. There was no sound from inside. Her heart hammered with excitement just thinking of all the things she could make with those rags.

She crept a bit closer and reached the gate. Peering through the iron bars, she could see it: a small pile of rags lying among the rubbish and filth. Of course, they'd need to be boiled again, which was dreadful, but at least the worst of May's itching had stopped. She'd just carry them with her arms out straight to stop the lice from jumping onto her body. Grasping the bars, she leaned back and gave the gate a sound pull.

Nothing happened.

May looked up at the gigantic lock, its keyhole like a screaming mouth above her head. It was locked.

Her shoulders sagged, and she looked longingly through the bars again. How could she reach them?

A scraping sound caught her attention. Looking up, she saw something on top of the wall to her left – hands. Hands, seizing the edge of the wall. And then, in a trice, a small figure was on top of the wall. She caught only a vague impression of scrawny legs and a pinched face glancing this way and that before it was dropping down off the wall and scampering across the grubby courtyard straight toward the rags.

"Hello," May called out.

The figure skidded to a halt, his head snapping around to stare at her, and she saw that it was a boy. He wasn't much older than she; his face was very pale, meanly pinched around the cheekbones, and his eyes glimmered from deep inside his skull. For a second, his muscles tightened, like he was about to spin around and bolt. Then he rushed forward.

"Hi there," May called again.

The boy ignored her. He was running for the rags. She cried out, stretching her arm through the gate as though she could grab them from him, but he'd already yanked them into his arms. Spinning around, he rushed back toward the wall, vaulted onto a rubbish bin and was back on top of the wall before she could blink.

"Wait," May cried.

Already, he was whisking over the wall. May bolted after him, her breath racing, the coins jingling in her pocket. But as she darted around the corner of the courtyard, the boy was already running down the alleyway as fast as his legs could carry him, clinging to the rags.

"Wait," she called again. "I don't want to hurt you."

He stumbled as he reached the mouth of the alley, slipping to one knee. May redoubled her pace, almost reaching him.

"I just want to be friends," she called out, despairingly.

He hovered at the end of the alley for a second, his eyes flashing up to hers. They were deep green, like emeralds, and filled with fear. For an instant, he hesitated. It seemed as though he would wait after all.

But then he clutched the rags more closely, lousy though they were, turned for the street and was gone.

MAY'S little hands were dancing over the fabric. Blanche could hardly believe that such tiny fingers were able to move so quickly, stitch after stitch falling into the bit of rag. Beside her lay a little stack of clothes she'd finished mending; Blanche always made sure she started with the mending, otherwise she'd do little else other than make tiny animals all day.

But the mending was done. Now, May was busy cutting the last stitch on her latest creation. She held it up to the light, and Blanche saw that it was a diminutive little dress, with holes for the arms and head, cobbled together from two bits of rag – one green, one red.

"What have you made there, poppet?" she asked, not moving from where she was making gruel for dinner. It had been gruel for the past three days; rent had been hard on them, and buying a few grubby rags from the rag-and-bone man had been even harder. But if May could sell a few toys tomorrow, things would be better.

"A little dress for the dolly," said May. She reached for the doll she'd made the night before – its body and limbs a collection of sausage-shaped lengths of fabric stuffed with rags – and tugged the dress on. To Blanche's increasing surprise, the dress fit perfectly.

"May, that's wonderful." She came a little closer. "You should ask thruppence for that one."

"Thanks, Mama." May gave her a brief smile, fingering the edge of the doll's dress. "I like her very much. I saw a little girl just like her on the street yesterday. Her papa bought the bird with the long tail feathers."

"That's nice, sweetheart." Blanche wondered if the man and his little girl would be looking for a tenement, then quickly dismissed the thought. No one with tuppence to spare for toys would want to come and live here. Still, she knew they desperately needed to find another family to share the room with.

Perhaps she could try talking to the Jacksons down the hall. She knew Mrs. Jackson had just been laid off from work, and perhaps they needed to save the money, even though squeezing the six Jackson children into the tiny tenement wouldn't be easy...

"Now I'm going to make a fox," said May happily, reaching for another bit of rag. "For the little boy who took the workhouse rags."

"What?" Blanche looked up from the gruel. "Why would you do that?"

May looked up at her, those blue eyes soft and luminous. "He looked sad and lonely, and scared and hungry, Mama."

"But he took your rags."

"They're nobody's rags," said May patiently, turning her attention back to her sewing. "And he seemed as though he was nobody's little boy, so I thought a little fox might cheer him up."

Blanche felt her eyes blur suddenly with tears and wondered just how much pride a heart could hold before it burst.

※

It took almost a week before May saw the little boy again.

She had been coming to the workhouse every time she was finished with selling her toys. Every other day, she would take all the toys she'd made the day before and sell them on the street while Mama took the mending to Mrs. Watson. And every time Big Ben tolled a quarter to four, she'd scamper to the workhouse and hide there, clutching the little fox in both hands.

He was beginning to grow rather scuffed and worn from all the squeezing by the end of that week, and May was wondering if she needed to make another fox when she saw him: the little boy, scampering down the alleyway, his eyes fixed on the wall in front of him. He looked thinner and hungrier than ever, the sharp angles of his shoulders jutting against his threadbare coat, and May longed to rush out and cheer him up.

Instead, she shrank deeper into her hiding place among some boxes, waiting for him to go past. It worked. He didn't see her; instead, he trotted right past her, ran up to the wall, and vaulted up onto it with a quickness that surprised her. Pausing for an instant, he glanced left and right, then disappeared over the other side of the wall.

This was her chance. May stepped out of her hiding place and stood squarely in the alley, holding the little fox tightly in both hands. A thrill of nervousness ran through her. Mama didn't like this idea, she knew; Mama was always telling her to stay away from boys in the street in case they pushed her down and took her money or beat her. But this little boy just didn't seem to be the kind who would do such a thing.

And she had made this fox just for him. She couldn't do anything else with it other than to give it to him.

There was no more time for indecision now, in any case. The little boy was appearing over the wall, quick as a cat, the rags in his arms. He was over the wall and running down the alley before he saw her and came skidding to a halt a few yards away. She braced herself, but he didn't seem inclined to take a step nearer, let alone push her down. His eyes darted around the alley, finding no escape.

"Hello," May said brightly.

Her voice was as cheerful and friendly as she could make it, but the boy still flinched back, glancing around nervously as though her words would bounce off the walls like a boomerang and hit him in the skull.

"I'm May," she said, holding up the fox. "I made this for you."

The boy watched her warily. For a second, he seemed to consider darting past her. Then his shoulders slumped a little.

"I saw you earlier. On Monday."

"That's right." May grinned. "You remember."

"You wanted to take the rags." The boy's hands tightened on them. "Well, you can't have them. I have to sell them to the rag-and-bone man, and you can buy them from him."

"Is that the only way you can get anything to eat?" May asked.

The boy said nothing, but the desperation in his eyes answered yes.

"I understand. Rags are important." May held out the fox. "This is for you. I made you a fox because you're so quick and clever."

The boy studied it, then clutched the rags more tightly. "I know this is a trick. You just want my rags."

"I do want rags, but I won't take yours. I just need some to make animals out of. Do you know where I can get more?"

"No. Get out of my way."

May shrugged. She bent down, setting the fox on the floor, and backed away. "Please take the fox. I can't give him to anyone else now, can I? He's for you."

The boy glanced at the fox, then at her, then at the space between them. Quickly, he slunk nearer, grabbed it, and scampered back a few steps. He gave her another suspicious look before turning the fox this way and that, inspecting it. Unexpectedly, she saw the corner of his mouth twitch in a smile.

"What's your name?" May asked.

He looked up, his shoulders sagging a little. "Taylor. Taylor Harris."

"Nice to meet you, Taylor." May smiled. "I suppose I'll see you some other time."

She turned to go, but his voice rang out clear and lovely behind her: "Wait."

May turned around.

The boy picked out a few small bits of rag from the bundle in his arms. "Old Rags don't pay well for the little ones. You can have 'em, if you want."

He tossed the rags in her direction, and May scooped them up gladly. "Oh, thank you," she said. "Thank you." She paused, looking up at the wall. "What does Old Rags give you for them?"

The boy glanced at the bundle in his arms. "For this much? Maybe sixpence."

"I sell these for tuppence." May nodded at the fox in his hands. "I could make a shilling and sixpence out of a huge big bundle like that, with enough time."

"You could?" The boy stared at her.

"Yes, but I can't get over the wall," said May. "And if I buy that many rags from the rag-and-bone man, he asks for more money than just sixpence. So I'd rather give my sixpence to you for climbing the wall."

The boy cocked his head a little to one side, eyes glittering as he considered her words.

"All right, then," he said. "Let's see your sixpence."

May tugged the coin from her pocket. She was so grateful that Mama had taken the time to teach her a little bit of arithmetic, even if it was rudimentary: all she really knew was that a sixpence was less than a shilling, and that a tuppence was less than a sixpence, and a penny was less than a tuppence.

"Here," she said, flicking it through the air toward him. He caught it effortlessly, and for an instant, she thought he might run away – rags and all.

But he didn't. He looked at her, and a smile played on his lips, and he held out the rags. "Thank'ee," he said.

"No, thank *you*," said May, immensely pleased. She took the rags, grinning up at him. "I'll see you here in two days' time."

"Two days," said Taylor. He paused. "And thank'ee for the fox."

Then he brushed past her, as though relieved to finally escape, and scampered down the street on his thin legs. But when he reached the mouth of the alleyway, he turned back for a moment, raised a skinny hand, and waved.

It was then that May knew she'd made a friend.

***

BLANCHE HAD no idea how May was managing to concentrate in this din. Two of the Jackson children were screaming at each other; the other two were just screaming, and Mrs. Jackson's voice was a sad and reedy attempt at order in the midst of a world enveloped in chaos. Blanche's head was splitting from the noise.

She stirred the rags she was boiling, letting out a sigh as she glanced over at May. Somehow, despite the chaos, her little girl was dutifully sewing a patch onto one of Mrs. Watson's housecoats. That, at least, made it possible for her to remind herself that the noise and chaos of having the entire Jackson family next door was worth it. Halving the rent had made their lives far easier again, and for once, they had more than enough coal to boil the rags and cook dinner at the same time.

"You know, darling," Blanche said, raising her voice to make herself heard over the screaming, "you really were very clever last winter when you started buying the rags from that little boy."

"Taylor's lovely, Mama," said May, not looking up from her sewing. "And he's always so very hungry. That poor little sixpence every second day is all he gets."

"I'm just glad you don't have to climb the wall, or put yourself at risk," said Blanche, shuddering at the very thought.

"Taylor's so quick. No one can catch him. He's over the wall in a trice, and that's it." May laughed. "But I keep telling him not to hold the rags so tightly. I'm so afraid he'll get lice too, Mama."

He's a street child. He's crawling with lice already, Blanche thought. "Well, I'm sure he's very grateful for the money we give him."

May lowered her sewing for a moment, looking up at Blanche. "It's not enough for rent, though, Mama. Is it?"

"I don't know," said Blanche, but it wasn't true. It was hardly enough for a few scraps of food; she knew it was nowhere near enough for any kind of rent. They could barely afford their own rent, after all.

"I wonder where he sleeps," said May. She gazed up at the window. "He won't ever say."

"Perhaps he lives in an orphanage," Blanche suggested.

"No, he doesn't. He grew up in one, but a family took him in, only they didn't do it for love. They just wanted him to work in their cotton mill. Then he got sick."

Blanche couldn't help feeling a tug on her heartstrings at those words. As a child herself, she'd lost friends to the horrors of brown lung.

"He's better now. Mostly," said May. "But still... it'll be winter soon, won't it, Mama?"

"Very soon, darling," said Blanche.

May looked up at her, and her blue eyes were suddenly brimming with tears. "Oh, Mama, what will poor Taylor do?"

"I suppose it won't be his first winter, sweetheart. He'll do whatever he did last winter."

"Last winter he still lived in the mill." The tears escaped, running down May's cheeks. "Oh, Mama, can't he come and stay with us?"

"No." The word snapped from Blanche's lips more sharply than she'd meant, and she saw May lean back in surprise at her tone, the tears flowing faster. "No," Blanche repeated, more gently this time, even though her body was trembling with fright at the very thought of being responsible for another person. "May, my dear, we're barely getting by as it is, just the two of us. Of course, Taylor can't stay with us."

May said nothing, wiping at her tears, but her cheeks were pale with shock at the tone Blanche had used. She turned her attention back to her sewing. Blanche let out a shaky breath, stirring the rags more vigorously.

She had never been the one to slam the door before.

THERE WAS NO WIND TODAY, but still Taylor pulled his tattered coat more tightly around himself as he walked, forcing his feet to move, forcing his leaden legs to keep going. The cold seemed to be seeping up from the earth itself, numbing his bare feet. He had seen the old men and women on the street who had toes missing. He wondered if all of his toes would make it through the coming winter.

He wondered if all of *himself* would make it through the coming winter.

He had just crawled out of his latest hiding place, underneath the hedge of a rundown old church. It was nowhere near as sheltered as the spot in the alley he'd had earlier, but some bigger boys had taken over the alley, and that was that. Taylor had been forced to run for his life. Even the old bit of blanket he'd had was left behind. Now he had nothing.

Nothing but the hope of seeing May – and getting a sixpence.

He probed hungrily in his coat pocket, digging out his last scrap of a bread crust. It had gone mushy and smelled dreadful when he raised it to his lips, but it was food, and he choked it down despite its sour taste. It would be enough to get him to the workhouse wall, he hoped. It would just have to be enough, even if his legs felt numb and useless under him, and he shivered with each step, hands in his pockets. With his right thumb and forefinger, he caressed the tiny, worn fox that went everywhere with him.

There was a sudden kiss of ice cold on his cheek. He slowed – he feared that if he stopped, he might never get moving again – and stared up at the leaden gray sky. Another snowflake drifted down, brightly white against the drab city. It landed on the payment and dissolved into nothing.

A shudder ran down Taylor's spine, and this time, it had nothing to do with the cold. The snow had come. Winter was here.

He quickened his pace, keeping his eyes fixed on the pavement in front of him, forcing his legs to move faster despite their dull ache that shot all the way up into his back and shoulders. As always, he found himself praying for the last block that she would be there. That this wouldn't be the day she let him down.

Of course, she was there. She was always there. When Taylor turned into the alley, she was standing by the wall, waiting, her golden curls dusted with flakes of white like stars upon a golden night. The sound of his footsteps made her turn around, that smile lighting up her brilliantly blue eyes. She seemed to be the only thing in the world that had colour, her cheeks rosy red against the gray day, her eyes brilliantly blue against the faded brickwork.

"Hello, Taylor," she whispered, not raising her voice too high for fear of attracting attention from the workhouse. Even her words seemed to hold more colour than the crashes and rattles and hisses of the city around them.

"Hello, May." Taylor smiled, his face stiff with cold.

"Isn't the snow pretty?" May smiled up at it, laughing as a few snowflakes settled on her cheeks.

"It is," said Taylor, but he thought she was the pretty one – perhaps even the prettiest thing he'd ever seen.

"I brought some bread." May dug in her pockets, pulling out a brown paper parcel that smelled absolutely wonderful.

Taylor's mouth immediately began to water, but he knew that if he hesitated any longer, they risked losing the rags altogether. And he couldn't survive without that sixpence. "I'll be right back."

"Be careful," May called.

Already Taylor was scrambling over the wall, a movement that had grown effortlessly familiar. He flitted across the courtyard, gratified to see that a larger than normal bundle of rags was lying in its usual spot. They must have had a lot of new intakes this week. Snatching it all up into his arms, he skipped out over the wall, landing easily on the other side.

"You're *so* clever," said May. "Shall we sit on the bridge with our bread?"

"Let's go," said Taylor.

Sitting on the bridge in the first place had been May's idea. Taylor didn't see why they should sit out in the cold when they could huddle in a shop doorway; in fact, at first, Taylor had only agreed to eat with May because he was hungry. Now, he found that eating with her was more about her and less about the food. He hadn't realized how hungry he had grown for more than just food, but for conversation, for laughter. For connection with someone.

He felt real again, and human, when he was sitting with May.

Now, he'd grown to see the charms of their spot on the bridge. They sat with their legs poking through the pillars of the railing, kicking their bare toes over the foul brown water where it splashed and foamed lazily against its litter-strewn banks. May tore the piece of bread in half, and Taylor gulped down his portion, forcing himself to take small bites. Making himself sick was a risk he couldn't take.

"Does your mama know that you bring me bread?" Taylor asked.

"No," May admitted. "But I suppose – well – it's my animals that make our money, so an extra h'pennyworth of bread could be mine, couldn't it?"

Taylor couldn't deny her logic, even if he worried about what Miss Eplett would say if she knew her daughter was spending their hard-earned pennies on feeding this street rat. Leaning against the pillar, he permitted himself to take another bite of the bread.

"Tell me about the animals you made this week," he said, simply wanting to listen to her voice.

"Oh. I made the most wonderful animals. I saw a picture of something called a lion in a bookshop window when I was trying out a new place to sell my toys. Have you ever seen a lion, Taylor?"

"No," said Taylor. "Except on the coat of arms. I didn't know they were real."

"They are real, it seems," said May. "They look like cats, but with long, fluffy manes. I made the loveliest lion, with two old buttons for eyes, a nice big cuddly one with strips of rags for a mane. I sold him for fourpence – and the little boy was so excited."

The joy in her voice made him smile. Sitting with her was like holding out his hands to a warm, crackling fire in the depths of his soul's winter.

"I would like to see a real lion," said Taylor. "It sounds so frightening. Are they very big?"

"I don't know. There was just a picture on the cover of the book. Mama said that it was a book about African animals. Do you know where Africa is?"

"I've no idea."

"It must be a wonderful place, with all those lions." May's voice grew dreamy, and she gazed down at the water as though it could tell her all the world's mysteries. "I would like to see Africa someday. Or just the country here."

"I would like to see the country, too," said Taylor. "I like horses."

"Horses?" May smiled up at him. "I'll make you a horse, someday. I've done lots."

"They're so beautiful and patient. I love the way they move, and their noses look so soft. I wanted to touch a coal-monger's horse once, but the coal-monger shouted at me."

"Well, I think we should find you another horse to touch," said May determinedly. She stood up. "Come on, Taylor. Let's find a horse."

"May – " Taylor began, but he knew that tone of voice; May had set her mind to something and would not be easily dissuaded.

"This way," she said, scampering off across the bridge.

Taylor groaned inwardly. Picking the last crumb from his lap and sucking it hungrily from his fingers, he got up and scooped up the rags, trotting after her.

"I see one, right over there." May cried, at the far end of the bridge, pointing. "Come on, Taylor."

She was laughing as she turned the corner off the bridge, and looking up at the horse, not down at her feet. That was why her foot caught on the step. That was why she fell forward, a cry of alarm bursting from her lips, pitching straight toward the cold and deadly waters of the Thames.

Taylor didn't think. His body acted of its own accord, flinging him forward, lunging to grab her. His arm smacked against the bridge's railing with a terrible impact that jolted pain through his entire body, but somehow his fingers had found the back of her dress, and he hauled her back, spinning them both onto the road.

"Watch out!" barked an angry gentleman as they nearly crashed into him.

"Taylor." May gasped, clutching his uninjured arm. "Oh – thank you. I nearly fell in." Her face was ashen with shock.

"Are you all right?" Taylor asked.

"I'm fine – oh. Your arm."

Taylor tried to lift it, but a pang of agony stopped him. When he looked down, bright blood was trickling down his forearm from the gash in his elbow, steaming in the cold air. The sight sent a terrible shock through his body. In street life, blood was death. He'd seen an old lady on the streets die from a much smaller wound than this; it had turned red, then ghastly yellow, then black. By then, she had been almost gone already, and had lain suffering in a gutter for days before the mercy of death finally came upon her.

"May," he croaked out, the fear making him dizzy.

May clutched his other arm. "It's all right, Taylor. It'll be all right."

"May." He looked up at her, his body trembling from head to toe. "I'm scared... I'm so scared."

"You don't have to be scared." May gripped his arm, then took a deep breath. "You're coming home with me."

She gathered up the scattered rags.

BLANCHE TIPPED the water from the pot and set it on the box they used as a kitchen table, peering into it. From its bottom, the pale, formless shape of a boiled cabbage seemed rather unprepossessing to her, but it was food, and it was hot – and these days, hot dinners had become routine. Her heart swelled with both pride and guilt at the thought of it. Pride of her sweet May and her skills; guilt, because in all her questing to care for her daughter, she had ended up being the one for whom her daughter cared. And poor May was only eight years old.

She gazed out of the tenement window at the bleakness of the street beyond. She could only see a tiny strip of muddy street and the close, bare brick wall of the neighbouring building. May should be growing up like Ludwig's other children, she thought. With a governess and a vast house and long, green lawns to play on. She should be expressing her creativity in embroidery with the most expensive silk and threads, not cobbling together stuffed animals for sale on the street using bits of old rag from the workhouse. A tear rolled down Blanche's cheek, and since May was still out, she allowed it to roll. It was the one luxury she could have at times.

If May had had a mother who wasn't a fool, who had married and settled down instead of carrying on a desperate affair, then perhaps she would have had the childhood she deserved.

The clatter of footsteps on the hallway outside their rooms made Blanche wipe the tear away quickly, even though it didn't sound like May – it sounded like two children. She couldn't let May see how sad she was. Turning away from the pot, she took out their tin bowls and began to set them on the kitchen table when she heard the hiss of the curtain being drawn aside.

"Mama, I'm home," May called.

Blanche turned, but the glad greeting died on her lips. May wasn't alone. She stood in the doorway, her cheeks flushed with triumph, her arm wrapped around the bony little shoulders of a boy who must have been a couple of years older even though he was about the same height that May was. He was little more than a bag of bones, wrapped in rags that draped miserably from his skeletal frame; his cheeks were pinched and ashen, and the only thing about him that seemed to hold any life or colour was his eyes. They were dark brown and held unspeakable fear.

This had to be Taylor.

Shock and terror washed over Blanche, dizzying her. She had only just worked out how to keep herself and May in food. What was she going to do now? Why had her daughter denied her like this?

"May," she said, her voice quivering, "what is this?"

"This is Taylor, Mama," said May. "I know you said no – but we were on the bridge, and then I was running, and I slipped and nearly fell in the river. And Taylor grabbed me and saved me, but he hit his arm on the railing."

Taylor said nothing. He had one hand clasped over the opposite elbow; Blanche could see dried blood between his fingers.

"Please, Mama, I couldn't just leave him out there." May's eyes were suddenly filled with tears. "I knew you'd be angry, but – oh, please, can he stay with us just one or two nights, until his arm feels better?"

Blanche stared at the boy. She had no reason to doubt May's story; her daughter could be defiant at times, but there was no dishonesty in her. If that was true, Taylor had saved May's life.

"I'm not angry, darling," said Blanche quietly. *I'm scared*, she added, but only to herself. "He can stay, but only two nights."

"Thank you, Mama, thank you, thank you." May ran to her, throwing her arms around Blanche's waist. Blanche kissed her daughter's head, then looked up at Taylor. The boy's shoulders were still set like he might bolt at any minute, but his eyes were suddenly aglitter with tears of relief.

"Thank'ee, ma'am," he whispered.

Blanche told herself that her heart didn't melt at those words. She told herself that she wasn't already falling a little in love with this poor street boy with his gentle eyes.

That was what she told herself, in any case.

PART III

CHAPTER 6

Two Years Later

May tied off the last stitch and held up her creation to the light, turning it this way and that. It was her first time making this creature, something she'd heard came from India; a kind of cat, covered in black and white stripes.

"What do you think, Mama?" she asked, holding it up.

Mama looked up from where she was boiling the last batch of rags. Their stench filled the room, a sweaty, sticky thing that seemed to cling to every surface in the little tenement – the two sleeping pallets in one corner, the curtain that was more threadbare than ever, the very walls themselves.

"I think those stripes are lovely, dear," she said. "How did you manage to make them?"

"I'm trying to embroider them." May sighed. "But I can't get them quite right. It's just that the charcoal doesn't last."

This was true; May had redrawn the charcoal face onto Taylor's little fox what felt like a hundred times over the past two years.

"The fine ladies I've seen always did their embroidery on a flat bit of cloth, not on something that was already made," Blanche offered. Not mentioning that the lady she'd mentioned was Mrs. Turner, the wife of May's father. "Perhaps you should embroider it first, and then sew it into a – whatever that is."

"It's called a tiger, Mama," said May. "I saw a stuffed one in the toy shop window and asked the proprietor."

"And he told you?"

"Oh, Mr. Drake isn't so bad." May laughed.

Blanche felt her mind spinning like a cog. Perhaps Mr. Drake could ultimately be persuaded to buy stock of some toys from May, she thought. She'd need better fabric. Better everything.

From behind the curtain, a series of dreadful coughs emanated from the Jacksons' part of the tenement. Blanche stirred the pot more vigorously, hoping that the splash of water would drown out the sound, but immediately May lowered the half-done tiger and cocked her head.

"Listen to that," she said. "Poor Sadie sounds terrible."

"I'm sure it's just a cold, dear," Blanche lied. She knew that the Jackson children worked in a cotton mill, and having lived in the slums for this long, she also knew brown lung when she heard it.

"I should make her something," May decided.

"You already gave her a sweet little cow, didn't you?"

"Yes, but I know she likes birds as well, Mama. I'll make her a nice bird to cheer her up."

Blanche sighed inwardly, staring down at the reeking rags as she boiled them. She didn't spend all this time on these disgusting rags just so that May could make things to give away. At the same time, how could she be angry? It was part of who her daughter was.

Footsteps sounded in the Jacksons' tenement, and a brief mumble of hello. Then the curtain rustled, and Taylor stepped into the room, shaking back a knot of damp hair from his forehead.

"I found some more," he announced, breathless with excitement.

Blanche couldn't help smiling at the boy as she turned to him. He had his arms clutched around a bundle of rags in all different colours; he glanced only briefly at her before turning his eyes on May, as if desperate for her approval. Taylor looked different these days. Taller, for one thing; and there was colour in his cheeks, too. Blanche didn't say so, for fear that May with her gentle heart would bring home another lost puppy like him, but it gave her joy to see how he'd grown.

And having a strong young boy around had proven useful, too.

"Oh, Taylor, they're perfect," May squealed with delight, jumping up from where she sat and fingering a strip of brightest yellow. "Look at this."

"Don't touch those, May. Taylor will help me boil them in a minute. These are almost done," said Blanche.

"Let me do that for you, Miss Eplett," said Taylor, hurrying to take the stick from her and setting the new rags carefully in a corner. "I can help."

"Thank you, dear," said Blanche.

The little boy began to stir, his face as studious as though this was the most important task in the world. And Blanche realized, then, that she had come to love him almost as much as May did.

MAY WAITED until Mama had gone out to fetch the mending before she took the little bird she'd sewn and slipped over to the curtain.

Mrs. Jackson wasn't home. She almost never was; it seemed as though whatever job she did at the factory – along with the four oldest children – took all day and some of the night, too. But as always, the two tiniest Jacksons were home. Emmy and Toby sat in the corner of the room, pushing a tattered ball made of rags tied together back and forth, their faces numb and blank as they did so, like soulless puppets pretending to be normal children.

Unlike normal, though, a third little Jackson was home – Sadie. She was lying on one of their two pallets, eyes closed, a tattered blanket drawn up to her face. May paused. Perhaps the little girl was asleep. She was no older than May herself, but her face was very pale, and the dark circles under her eyes made her look ancient. Like a dried-up old skull. May wondered if she looked like that, too. She wondered if there were times when Sadie's hands also ached and cramped, the way May's did, and if her eyes were also sore and tired like May's were at the end of a long day when she picked stitches together by the faltering candlelight.

Hesitant, May backed away, not wanting to wake little Sadie. Then Toby pushed the makeshift ball a little too hard and it bumped against Emmy's belly. The toddler threw back her head and let out a thin, wailing cry, a repetitive thing, the kind of cry that did not expect to be heard.

Sadie sat up, the movement wresting another series of wretched coughs from her. "Stop that," she wheezed. "Emmy, stop."

"It's all right." May hurried over, the way she always longed to do when Emmy cried, and scooped the toddler into her arms. Emmy must have been three years old, but she was light as a bird in May's arms, like a bag of bones with skin instead of feathers. She immediately stopped crying, pulling back to stare at May almost in shock, her greasy hair hanging around her thin face like bits of string.

"You're all right, pet," said May.

Emmy stared at her, her nose running in yellow strings over her top lip. It made May feel queasy, so she gently put the child down, and Emmy went straight back to shoving the ball back and forth with Toby. It was strange to watch them, silent and mechanical as they were. She wondered if all children were like this. She thought she had been a little noisier, when she was that age.

"Don't mind Emmy. She's just – fussing." Sadie paused for breath between words, like a whole sentence was too much for her.

May came over to the sleeping pallet and sat down carefully on the floor beside Sadie. "Are you sick?" she asked.

"Of course, I'm sick." Sadie closed her eyes. "Or I'd be at work."

"I'm sorry."

"Well. That's how it goes."

It seemed strange to hear Sadie speak with such bitterness, considering that she wasn't much older than May herself. Perhaps as old as Taylor.

"I'm sure you'll be better soon," said May quietly.

Sadie said nothing.

May held out her hand, palm up, fingers closed. "I made something for you."

"I know. I still have it," murmured Sadie. "A cow. Under my pillow."

"No – I mean, I made you something new," said May.

Sadie's eyes fluttered open. "Did... did my – mama ask you?"

"No, I just..." May stopped as Sadie's face fell.

The older girl turned her head away. "I thought perhaps – Mama had – well, never mind."

"Please." May stretched her arm out a little further. "It's just for you."

Sadie turned her head back, her eyes fluttering open, and May opened her fingers to reveal a tiny bird sitting in the palm of her hand. She'd used strips of the yellow rags Taylor had brought for her to make it look like it had long, feathered wings, like a firebird.

"Oh, it's – beautiful." Sadie's breath caught in her chest. She reached out a skeletal hand, lifting the bird from May's palm, and a coughing laugh escaped her.

"I hope you feel much better soon, Sadie," said May.

Sadie said nothing. She was looking at the bird, stroking its bright rags, as though her eyes were starving for colour.

As though nothing else in her whole world was beautiful.

CHAPTER 7

EVEN AFTER TWO YEARS, Taylor still found it a little strange to be walking the street in the cold wind and *not* feeling it directly on his skin. Of course, it still nipped at the bottom of his ears, and his lips and chin, and his cheeks – everywhere that his long coat didn't reach. But with its collar turned up to his jaw, and its buttons all done up, and with the way it hung all the way down to his knees, the coat was like a shield against the wind.

It had once been part of the rags Taylor had rescued from the workhouse. Miss Eplett had wanted to cut it up, but May had argued passionately that it would fit him, if she just took it in here and added a button there – and so she had, magically changing something useless and discarded into something good and important. She had a way of doing that, May did.

And now it hugged him, and the wind couldn't get in, and Taylor practically felt like skipping down the street. Food every day, a warm coat, a roof to sleep under, people who cared for him – even if Miss Eplett didn't always want to admit it. It was everything he had ever dreamed of.

The thought was more than enough to counteract the wave of dread that washed through him as he stepped out of the maze of streets and onto the docks themselves. The smell of fish and tar filled the air; there was a gentle hiss of water against the crumbling piers, and the shouts of sailors, the creaking of ropes, the slap of damp canvas as sails were taken down and unrolled. Every time he'd come here, Taylor had been rebuffed. He had only ever been offered work once – as a cabin boy, for his keep, and that wasn't enough for him. He wanted – *needed* – to bring back something to May and Miss Eplett.

Squaring his shoulders, he braced himself against the tides of doubt and rejection that seemed to greet him anywhere he went and stepped forward. He hadn't tried the shipwright on the northern side of the docks yet. It was as good a place as any.

The shipwright was a vast, vigorous man, towering like a mainmast over the scrambling mess of laborers who seemed to be busy stripping down a ship to its very bones; hauling off barnacle-encrusted planks with a crackle of tar and a splintering of wood. Taylor thought the ship looked sad and lifeless with its skeleton jutting out against the grey sky. It moaned quietly in the wind as he walked up to the shipwright, taking a deep breath to fortify himself. Miss Eplett had gotten work cleaning fish a few times here. If she could, then surely so could he.

"Excuse me, sir," he said, using the clipped tones that May always had when she spoke to customers.

The shipwright turned, his piercing blue eyes resting on Taylor, and let out a booming laugh that could knock over a horse at fifty paces. "Hark at the lad." he roared. "What are ye, a li'l gennulman o' some kind?"

Taylor swallowed. "Just a boy looking for work, sir. Any kind of work."

"I don't have work for a scrap like you. A puff o' wind would blow you o'er. Or a big enough swallow." The shipwright waved a dismissive hand. "Be off w' ye."

Taylor knew better than to press his luck, but he did it anyway. "Sir, please..."

The shipwright turned toward him again, the crags of his brows buckling under the weight of his displeasure. "I said, go away," he rumbled.

Taylor turned away, his shoulders slumping. It was the same everywhere he went. He wasn't big enough, wasn't strong enough, clever enough, fast enough. Not *enough*.

He wondered if he hadn't been enough to his mother, either. If that was why she had left him on that doorstep and sentenced him to a life without family.

His thin fists clenched. Only he *did* have a family now, and he was going to do right by them, whatever it took. Heading down the docks, Taylor scanned the faces of the men nearby, looking for someone who seemed approachable or at least vaguely less drunken and angry than everyone else.

He was contemplating a pair of fishermen hauling great barrels of fish from their boat when a whiff of something delicious rose through the putrid air. Bread – *fresh* bread. Turning, he followed the smell almost by instinct, moving from the docks to the street that ran right alongside them. Most of the buildings here were brothels and taverns, selling pleasure or fishing tackle or ropes to the men of the docks, but Taylor supposed they had to eat, too. So, there was a bakery on the corner, the baker just setting out a series of golden loaves in the window.

His hands clenched even tighter. He might not be clever or strong, but he *was* quick on his feet. His stomach churned at the thought of what Miss Eplett and May would think of him if they knew how regularly he did this, but at least he could bring something home to them, earn his keep just a little. Make up for the kindness they had shown him.

If he didn't, maybe they wouldn't let him stay.

He moved closer, casually, his head bowed as though he was staring at his feet where they moved along the pavement, but really his eyes were fixed upon that bread. The sign outside the bakery was still turned to "Closed." He could recognize that word. Any minute now, the baker would have to step outside to change it, and that would be his chance. The door would open then for a half second – and a half second was all Taylor needed.

Laying the last loaf in its place, the baker reached for the doorknob. Taylor was right there. As the man moved out of the shop, Taylor shot forward, squeezed his tiny frame past him, and then his hands were closing around two scalding loaves.

"Oi!" thundered the baker.

He turned, but Taylor was already slipping out again under his arm. With a roar of fury, the baker lunged at him. Taylor ducked, his bare feet slipping for a moment on the pavement; fingertips brushed across his back, but he regained his footing in a smooth movement and bolted.

"OI! STOP THIEF!" bellowed the baker.

But before the nearest bobby could hear, Taylor was up on a rubbish bin, over a wall and safely away, quick as a fish in the river.

At least he was good at *something*, even if it was something shameful.

BLANCHE'S bare hands stung from the biting cold of the air outside. A thick fog lay over London; she had felt as though she was fighting through it all the way home from another trip to Mrs. Watson's, like it was something physical holding her back. Her dress was shiny with damp filth as she clumped up the stairs to the top floor of the building where they lived. That same damp seemed to have found its way into her bones themselves, curling up in her joints in the form of ice crystals that grated painfully with every step she took.

But she was home now. She loosened her grip a little on her bundle, half expecting her fingers to crackle like breaking ice. Pushing open the door, she stepped into the Jacksons' half of the tenement, her eyes darting immediately to the sleeping pallet with a fearful jerk. For the last week, every time she stepped into the tenement, she both hoped and feared she would find poor Sadie lying dead. Feared, because the child had been like sunshine once, and was now only a husk of humanity; hoped, because then at least poor May would not have been the one to find her.

Instead, her eyes found Mrs. Jackson, sitting in a huddled heap on the pallet, her face covered with the wrung-out and reddened hands of a cotton piecer, her shoulders quivering with grief.

Blanche staggered to a halt. Mrs. Jackson, crying? She had never seen any emotion at all on the face of this woman.

Raising six children alone in a London slum seemed to have scrubbed her clean of all feeling. But she was crying now, very quietly, ignored by the children. And why was she home? Why were they *all* home?

A terrible suspicion grew in Blanche's belly, and her heart faltered at the thought. She set down the bundle and went over to the trembling woman, crushing her empathy with all of her strength. Her heart might sting for Mrs. Jackson now, but she wouldn't let anything harm May.

"Mrs. Jackson?" she said.

The woman flinched as though struck. Her worn hands fell from her face, and she stared up at Blanche with red eyes, tears streaming down her wrinkled cheeks.

"Miss Eplett," she whispered.

"What is it?" asked Blanche. Her eyes darted to the pallet. Sadie lay there, her face blue, breathing in tiny, rattling gasps. "Is it Sadie?"

"Oh, no. No... it's not Sadie." Mrs. Jackson reached out, her fingertips barely brushing the lump under the blanket where the child lay. Sadie made no response to the light touch. "Poor mite. She'll be out of this world tonight, God willing, and may the Lord keep her poor soul the way I could never keep her body." Mrs. Jackson spoke without emotion. "She'll be well out of this world."

Her words chilled Blanche to the bone. *Please*, she prayed silently. *Please may things never become so dire that I feel this way about my own child... that she'd be better off dead.*

Mrs. Jackson's quiet despair sucked at her like gravity, making her want to flee back to her little corner and escape. But she had to be heartless now, for May's sake. She squared her shoulders, clutched her bundle a little more tightly, and came straight to the point.

"Mrs. Jackson, have you lost your job?"

Mrs. Jackson looked up at her. There was no shock in her eyes, even though Blanche felt that slapping her in the face would have held less cruelty than those words at this moment.

"Yes," she said. "Me and all my kids. They took a lash to Robyn." She reached toward her second-to-youngest daughter. "They're all too quick to do it... I spoke up. Why did I speak up?" Another tear tipped quietly down her cheek.

Again, Blanche braced herself as though she was about to deal out a physical blow. "So how are you going to pay the rent, come Monday?"

The lack of surprise. The lack of flinch in Mrs. Jackson's voice; the total lack of emotion. "I can't."

Terror sucked at Blanche like she'd just run full speed onto a lake of thin ice. She could feel herself slipping, losing control, hear the creak of the ground breaking up beneath her feet, threatening to plunge her into freezing darkness. Things were hard enough as they were, now she had Taylor to feed, but at least they could eat daily. And if the rent doubled...

There was no way.

"Then I have to ask you to leave," said Blanche.

Mrs. Jackson looked up at her again. This time, there was a mute plea in her eyes.

"Please, Mrs. Jackson." Blanche crumpled up her empathy and tamped it down somewhere deep inside. "Rather leave now before the landlord evicts you."

Mrs. Jackson's shoulders fell. She said nothing. Neither did Blanche. She had done what she had to do, and she turned and walked back to her tenement and her child, the child for whom she would do anything.

Even this.

CHAPTER 8

May was really excited about this one. She had kept it hidden in her pocket all morning so Mama wouldn't see it; Mama could be so strange about her giving away things, and she didn't understand why. But she was bent on giving this away. It was far too special to sell. Some things just couldn't be given a price tag.

And the little mouse was one of them. She'd made mice before, but they'd never come out so perfect, with such a perfect, pointy muzzle tied off at the end and coloured black with charcoal to make a quivering nose; with draping bits of string for whiskers; with a long, plaited tail. He was friendly and comical to look at, and his button eyes were so bright that it seemed to May as though any moment he would sit up and run his paws over his whiskers.

He was perfect for little Emmy, she just knew it, and she knew the bear she'd made for Emmy had fallen apart last week (amidst much crying). The mouse would be perfect for her.

The moment Mama had gone, leaving Taylor to boil up the new rags while May got started on some new animals, she jumped down from her makeshift chair. She slipped the mouse from its hiding spot in her pocket and trotted eagerly over to the curtain.

"Where are you going?" Taylor asked, looking up from the pot.

"Just next door." May giggled. "Don't worry."

"May, maybe you shouldn't," said Taylor. "Sadie…"

"Sadie's sleeping," said May. "She'll be better soon. I just know it."

"May…"

"I'll be back in a moment, Taylor. It's all right."

Ignoring his protests, May brushed the curtain aside, her eye immediately catching Emmy where she was huddling in a corner, picking silently at the hem of her dress, her eyes red from crying as usual. She stepped forward, and then a giant, bare foot slammed down into the ground right in front of her, making her leap back in surprise with a squeal of shock.

"What are you doing?" Mrs. Jackson thundered.

May scrabbled backward. Why was Mrs. Jackson home? She hadn't heard a peep from her all day. Staring up at her, she realized with a shock that she hadn't heard a peep from any of them all day. They'd been here the whole time, but silent.

Her heart sank. Was it Sadie?

"I... I..." she stammered.

"Be off with you." roared Mrs. Jackson.

"Please, ma'am," May managed, holding up the mouse like a shield. "I just wanted to give Emmy something."

Mrs. Jackson's eyes narrowed. Then, to May's shock, her lower lip seemed to tremble. It was as surprising as seeing a mountain crack in half. Her face crumpled, and she turned away, her voice broken.

"If only you got your kind heart from your mother," she cried.

May stared at her. "But – I did."

"If that was true, she wouldn't be throwing us on the streets," sobbed Mrs. Jackson.

May stared at her, clutching the mouse, startled. She'd seen plenty of people shout at Mrs. Jackson, even Mama, and yet the big woman never cried. It was as though kindness pierced all the defences that cruelty never could.

"Please, Mrs. Jackson, my mama would never do such a thing," she said.

Taylor had come through the curtain. He grabbed her arm. "May, let's go back inside."

"But it's not true. Taylor, it can't be true. Mama would never put them on the streets – not with poor Sadie sick, and – "

"May, just leave it alone." Taylor tugged at her arm. "Come on."

Protesting, May was almost dragged back into the tenement, the little mouse still clutched in her arms. It had been shocking to see Mrs. Jackson cry.

But what was all the more shocking was that Mama had made it happen.

***

MAY DIDN'T KNOW how to speak to Mama when she came home a few hours later, her face pale and drawn with exhaustion, dark circles underneath her eyes. She was carrying a fresh bundle of mending for May, and as soon as she pushed the curtain aside, her weary eyes flashed to where May was sitting on the floor, packing up the day's work to be sold tomorrow afternoon.

For a moment, Mama just stood in the doorway, the bundle in her arms, her eyes expectant. Normally, May would leap up and run across the floor to her mother with a joyous cry. But that cry seemed to die in her throat; she just stared up at

Mama, thinking of the Jacksons, and her heart stung at the thought.

Realizing that May wasn't going to run to her, Mama set down the bundle and tried her best to smile. "Hello, my love," she said.

Poor Mama. She sounded so tired, yet the love in her voice was so genuine. It all didn't make sense. May couldn't resist getting up and going over to Mama, wrapping her arms around her mother's waist and holding her tightly.

"Darling, whatever is the matter?" Mama stroked her long hair.

"I don't understand, Mama," May whispered, tears gathering in a tight knot in her throat.

"What do you mean?"

"Oh, Mama, do you love me?"

"May." Mama's voice trembled with shock. She bent down, and even though May was much too big for this, she somehow managed to scoop her into her arms and hug her tightly to her chest. Mama sank down onto a box they used as a chair, cuddling May as though she were a baby. "I love you with everything in me, my sweetheart. I would do anything for you, anything." She sounded like she was about to cry. "Why would you ask me this?"

May buried her face in Mama's neck. She knew that Mama loved her, had always known it, and yet nothing felt right. "Did you really tell the Jacksons to leave, Mama?"

Mama's body froze. She drew back, her hands on May's shoulders, and her eyes were cautious. "I had to, darling. You have to understand that I don't have a choice."

"Don't have a choice?" May gasped. "Of course, we have a choice. They could just stay here."

"No, my love, they can't." Mama blinked fast, as though trying to hide her tears. "Mrs. Jackson has lost her job."

"I wondered about that," said Taylor quietly. He'd been sitting by the string across the back of the room, hanging up the rags he'd boiled earlier today. "It seemed strange that she'd be home with all of the older children."

"So she can't pay the rent anymore?" May asked.

"That's right, darling. Which means we'd have to pay the full rent." Mama shook her head. "We'd just been starting to do a little better, May. Don't you remember what it was like when we had no money? When we could only eat every two or three days, and hardly had a stick of coal to warm ourselves with?"

May's eyes burned with tears. "But what about the Jacksons, Mama? With no work and no home... why, they'll have nothing. They'll be on the streets, freezing cold, and hungry all the time... why can't we help them like we helped Taylor?"

Mama glanced up at Taylor, who ducked his head quickly, as though he was much too busy with the rags to be listening.

"Taylor's different," Mama said eventually.

"But can't we help them, Mama?" May begged, clutching the front of Mama's dress. "Please, please, can we help them? I don't want them to be starving and freezing. Oh, Mama, how could you do this?"

Mama hung her head, as though absolutely exhausted, her shoulders sagging. May felt a pang of guilt.

"Please, Mama, I'll make more animals. I'll make more – everything," May whispered. "I'll do anything. Please just help the Jacksons. Give them one more week."

Mama raised her head, and she was even paler than before. "All right," she said. "One more week, but that's all, May. I'm sorry, my love, but I can't help everyone. I'm doing my best as it is."

"Thank you, Mama." May flung her arms around her mother's neck. "Oh, thank you, thank you."

As Mama hugged her back, she saw that Taylor's head was bowed. As though he, too, was carrying some great weight.

CHAPTER 9

May's lips were blue, but somehow still curved in a smile. She was holding a little stuffed cow in her hands – a rotund creature, with a bit of old felt for a tail, and soft fabric horns that flopped over its embroidered eyes – and she held it up over her head, her cheerful voice wobbling only slightly even though her teeth chattered with cold.

"Pretty gifts. Stuffed animals. Toys for your children," she called out. "Get your toys here. Only tuppence each."

Taylor kept a sharp eye on the streets, his voice far less passionate as he held up a stuffed bear and called out, "Bears and birds. Dogs and cats. Something for everyone."

Miss Eplett had told May that Taylor always had to come with her when she was selling her animals so that she'd have a second set of lungs to cry her wares. In reality, she'd taken Taylor aside and begged him to keep an eye on her daughter. There were so many people out on these streets who would do unspeakable things to such a pretty young girl.

And she *was* pretty. Her great blue eyes glittered like jewels in the grey London day, filling the world with colour and beauty. The thought of anyone abusing that sweet innocence was enough to make Taylor's heart burn. He moved a step closer to her, determined not to let anything happen to her.

Movement. Someone in the crowd was coming toward them. Taylor's body clenched with fear, and he curled his small hands into fists – and what exactly was he going to do with them? He was hardly any bigger than May herself, a pathetic weed of a creature, and he knew there was nothing he could really do.

Taylor knew that if someone wanted to hurt May, he couldn't stop them. The thought made a feeling of utter helplessness wash over him. It clutched at his chest, his throat, and he was ready to scream –

Then a small girl emerged from the crowd, giggling, one hand held out toward the cow in May's hands. Her free hand was wrapped tightly around the finger of a tall, stooped man in a well-patched coat.

"Look at it, Uncle Ron." She was gasping. "Just look."

May let the little girl touch the cow with her fingertips, and she looked up at her uncle with wide, shining eyes.

"Only tuppence each, sir," said May eagerly.

"Tuppence?" The man rooted in a pocket. "Well, I suppose it *is* your birthday, Janey."

As the little girl began to squeal in excitement, Taylor closed his eyes for a second, letting the fear slowly leave his body. It was the same every day. He knew there was nothing he could really do to help May, no matter what she or Blanche thought.

When he opened his eyes, the girl had gone, and May was bending down stiffly to pick up another of her stuffed animals. There were only a few left; she selected a duck, holding it up in the air, her tired voice trembling as she cried out again, "Pretty gifts. Get your toys."

There was a distant rumble of thunder, and Taylor looked up at a sky stained black with coming rain.

"Don't you think it's time we went inside, May?" he asked her.

She lowered the duck, giving him a smile that was breathtakingly brilliant despite the harsh, exhausted circles under her eyes.

"Just a few more minutes," she said. "I just want to sell one more toy. We need some more money."

Taylor's stomach tightened as May went on crying her wares. He knew exactly why they needed that money, remembering her conversation with Miss Eplett last night. *I can't help everyone. I'm doing my best as it is*, Miss Eplett had said.

Taylor had known that May's mother had been talking about him, and the dreadful burden he was causing their family. His eyes rested on poor little May, on her skinny arms, the paleness of her cheeks. When they finally went back to the tenement, he knew that there would be no rest for May. She would get started on the mending right away and work until nine or ten o' clock tonight.

It didn't seem fair. It *wasn't* fair. May deserved so much better.

Taylor closed his eyes and prayed with all his heart that he'd find work soon.

THE RAIN that had been threatening yesterday afternoon was pouring down in sheets now. Taylor tried to keep to the overhangs of buildings as he made his way through the streets, his hands tucked deep inside his pockets, his neck drawn down into his collar. Ducking from one overhang to the next, a burst of icy rain gushed down the back of his shirt, and he shuddered at the cold.

But it wasn't the rain that was making his throat tighten as though filled with tears. It was this day, and the dreadfulness of it. Taylor had given up on the docks; today he was going from one door to the next, knocking on each, pleading for work. He had gained no jobs, only a few cuffs and curses for his trouble.

Perhaps this place would be different. He thought of May's shining optimism and tried to emulate it, telling himself this might be the shop that gave him work at last. He squared his shoulders, smoothed down his wet hair, and pushed the door open.

It was a pawnshop, Taylor saw, with rows of cubicles where people could have some privacy as they pawned or sold their goods. He wished he had something to sell. Instead, he walked up to one of the empty cubicles, and the man behind the counter gave him a sharp look.

"Pawn or sale?" he grunted.

"Neither, sir." Taylor tried to pronounce each word carefully, like May did; grownups loved that. "I'm here to ask if you need any help."

"Help?" the man grunted. "From an imp like you?"

Taylor had been called worse things today. "I'm hardworking, sir. I'll do anything. I'll scrub floors, I'll – "

"Be off with you," barked the man. "I've employed enough 'hardworking' scalawags like you to know that you're all up to no good."

Taylor felt a wave of desperation wash over him. He thought of May, of Miss Eplett, the Jacksons – all people who would benefit if he could just get this job.

"Sir, please, I'm begging you, just give me a chance," he pleaded. "I'll work for a penny a day. For a penny every second day. I just – "

"I told you to leave," snapped the man. "Now will you go, or shall I set my dogs on you?"

Taylor's eyes stung with tears. He backed away, then turned and crashed out of the shop and onto the pavement outside. His momentum carried him out into the street itself, the rain pouring down onto his face, his hair, drenching him to the bones.

With all his heart, Taylor wanted to scream at the injustice of it all. He watched as a man swept along the street, working his broom in quick, methodical motions. There was a girl in the window of the nearby grocer's shop, scrubbing the floors on her hands and knees. A little footman stood by a waiting carriage in the rain, shivering in his livery.

Taylor felt envious of every single one of them. At least they could contribute to something. At least they weren't relying on a poor little girl working hours and hours every day to keep them alive.

"Oh, May." Taylor covered his face with his hands, unable to hold back a sob. "How can I keep on doing this to you?"

He thought of her labouring away by the light of a stubby candle, of her blue eyes turning bloodshot from the work, of the way her small hands trembled at the end of a long day, and the thought of going back to them was unbearable. How could he tell them that he hadn't found any work, yet again? How could he look Miss Eplett in the eye?

There was only one thing to do, even though it tore Taylor's heart in half to do it. He could never have done it for anyone in the world except for May.

He turned and walked down the street, into the driving rain, and away from the tenement building that held the only people he'd ever truly loved.

"Mama, where is he?" May pressed her face against the tiny window, her eyes searching up and down the street. The rain had stopped, but damp still hung in a misty curtain over the city; it was hard to see very far, and her eyes strained with the effort. The streetlamp on their corner did little other than to cast a ball of frosted gold light around it. She squinted at it, hoping that any moment now, Taylor's slender silhouette would emerge from the mist.

"I'm sure he's on his way right now, my darling," said Mama, stirring a pot of gruel on the fire. Its smell was ordinary and tasteless, but May's stomach still rumbled at it. Yesterday had been Monday, rent day, and they had had nothing to eat all day long.

"But what's taking him so long? It's so dark, Mama. You always tell him not to stay out after dark." May sighed, peering outside again. "He's never done this before."

Mama lifted the pot from the fire and set it on their makeshift table, then came to join May at the window. "I don't know, darling. But Taylor's a big boy." She put a hand on May's shoulder, but it was trembling. "I'm sure he's all right. Maybe he's found work. Maybe he needed to stay late to finish his first day."

"But what if he's not?" May turned to Mama, her eyes stinging with tears. "Oh, Mama, what if he was knocked down on the street? Or fell into the river? Or what if he's sick, and can't walk home?" The terrible possibilities crushed her lungs as in a vice, and she began to sob, great hiccups of terror that threatened to tear her apart.

"May, May, my darling, it's all right." Mama wrapped her arms around her. "It's going to be all right." But May heard the fear in Mama's voice.

The distant tolling of a small church bell reached them, and May listened, counting. "Mama, it's nine o' clock." The thought sent a terrible thrill of fear through her. "Something has to be wrong. He should have been back by now." Her words dissolved again into sobbing. "He should have been back by now."

"He should." Mama was trembling. "Let's – let's go look for him, darling." She stood, and May scrambled to her feet, rushing to pull her coat over her shoulders.

"Stay close," said Mama, taking a firm grip of May's hand. "Did he tell you where he was going today?"

"To the docks, I think," said May.

They stepped out into the dark night, and May immediately felt a chill creep over her shoulders. She had never been outside so late before. She had half expected the city to be quiet; instead, it echoed with distant sounds. Bursts of laughter. Scrabbling in the gutters – rats? May hated rats. She stuck closer to Mama as they left the bubble of warm light from the streetlamp and advanced in the greyish dusk of the street; May had to keep her eyes fixed on the next streetlamp in order to be brave enough to keep going.

"Taylor!" Mama called out.

"Taylor!" May echoed.

Their voices bounced back at them from the towering buildings on either side, hollow and empty. And though May strained and strained her ears for that warm, familiar voice, Taylor didn't answer.

May added one more stitch, then sat back, holding up her latest creation to the light. Her sewing needle flashed faintly in the dim candlelight, dangling from the embroidered, smiling mouth of the bunny in her hands. It was a beautiful thing, its tail a pom-pom made of strips of rags, its welcoming smile and bright button eyes filled with joy.

A flicker of warmth wobbled in May's heart, then faded. Even her beautiful bunny couldn't bring her much joy herself. Not since Taylor was gone.

Mama and May had spent hours that night scouring the city for him, calling into dark alleyways, shouting his name up and down the streets. They'd slept just a few hours before Mama had headed out again, leaving May to continue her work. And that night, again, they'd searched and searched. But there was just no sign of him anywhere. Mama said that perhaps he'd found work somewhere and would come back when he'd finished it. Maybe he'd even gone out to sea, she said.

The thought of Taylor being gone at sea for months and months was unbearable enough. But far worse was the way that Mama had stared down into the dark water at the edge of the docks, and the way that the colour had drained from her face when she did so.

Mama looked pale even now, a week after Taylor had disappeared, as she folded up the newly mended clothes and packed them into a bundle to take them back to Mrs.

Watson. Her eyes were distant, and reddish. May had felt Mama's trembling against her when she cried herself to sleep each night. It was so hard to have her heart broken in three pieces; one for Taylor, one for Mama, and one for herself, without Taylor.

Tying off the bundle with a scrap of dirty string, Mama turned to May, and from the set of her shoulders May knew she was going to say something she didn't like. She opened her mouth, as if seeking the words, then stared at the rabbit in May's hands instead. "Oh, honey, it's lovely. Your best yet."

"Thank you," said May. She stroked the rabbit's soft, floppy fabric ears. "I'll see if I can get thruppence for him tomorrow." The thought of selling her animals alone, like she'd done yesterday, was hateful.

Mama wrapped her arms around May's shoulders and kissed the top of her head. "I'm proud of you, sweetheart. I don't know how you're managing to keep working even with – well, everything."

May looked up at her, startled. "What else could I do, Mama?" she said. "I love making these. It makes me happy... especially in a time like this." She blinked back tears.

"I'm glad there's something that makes you happy, darling." Mama's arms tightened around her. "May, honey, there's something I have to tell you."

"Yes, Mama?"

"I told you I would give the Jacksons two more weeks to find work, didn't I?"

Dread coiled in May's belly. "They'll find work soon, Mama. I just know it."

"I hope so, dear, but you must know that I can't give them more time." Mama's voice cracked, and she hugged May more closely. "Please, darling, don't be angry. I'm just trying to do what's best for you. Without Taylor fetching the rags for us, we have to buy rags to make your animals. Everything is harder now... I can't keep paying the Jacksons' rent, too."

Without Taylor. Those two words were enough to defeat any fight May might have wanted to put up on behalf of the Jacksons. She lowered her head, tears running down her cheeks.

"All right, Mama," she whispered.

"I'm so sorry, darling." Mama kissed her head, her voice broken. "I'm so sorry."

She picked up the bundle and hurried out of the room, leaving May alone at her makeshift sewing desk. May allowed the tears to keep running down her cheeks. What could she do to help the Jacksons?

Her eye caught some of the rags Mama had bought. They were larger than normal. Some of them were almost whole shirts, just with great holes in them.

An idea grew in May's mind. She climbed down from her seat and went over to the rags, turning them this way and that.

There was one last thing she could do for the Jacksons, after all.

CHAPTER 10

Blanche wished she could shake the unbearable heaviness in her chest. It felt like her heart had been replaced by some great leaden ball, dragging her down.

She'd taken Taylor in to make May happy, nothing more. But now that he was gone, she knew her sorrow weighed more heavily than just empathy for poor May's broken little heart. And now she was about to break poor May's heart once again.

She didn't look up as she walked through the Jacksons' portion of the tenement. She hadn't said a word to Mrs. Jackson since yesterday morning, when she'd reminded her that she needed to take her family and leave today. Mrs. Jackson had received the news in a simmering silence; Blanche couldn't wait for them to be gone. Truth be told, she'd grown tired of them, and she'd already found another family willing to share the tenement.

As she approached the curtain, a corner of Blanche's heart allowed her to hope Taylor had found his way home. That when she pulled the curtain aside, he'd be in the corner, boiling rags, and he'd turn around with that sweet gratitude on his face and say, *Hello, Miss Eplett*, in that gentle, respectful voice of his...

"Miss Eplett." Mrs. Jackson's voice was uncharacteristically gentle. "You'll take good care of that little girl now, won't you?"

Almost at the curtain, Blanche whipped around, indignation rising in her throat like bile. "I beg your pardon?" she gasped.

But there was nothing sharp or sarcastic in Mrs. Jackson's eyes. Instead, they were filled with gentleness, even — to Blanche's astonishment — tears.

"She's special, you know," said Mrs. Jackson. "There's no one else like her, not in this harsh old world. Keep her that way."

"I..." Blanche swallowed, not understanding. Then her eyes rested on the coat Mrs. Jackson was wearing. Last time Blanche had seen her, she'd been wearing the same threadbare coat she'd had for years, the one that tied around her belly with string and didn't seem to offer much more shelter from the elements than a wet paper bag. But now, Mrs. Jackson wore a snug, well-fitted coat, with big buttons down the front, and many patches across the back and shoulders.

Fury roared in Blanche's heart. "Mrs. Jackson," she gasped. "How could you. You've not paid a bent penny in rent for the past two weeks, but you have the money for a new coat?"

Mrs. Jackson's eyes narrowed. "I'm trying to thank you, you stupid hussy," she barked. "Don't make accusations against me."

Then one of the Jackson children, Toby, tugged at Blanche's sleeve. "May gave them to us, Miss Eplett," he said.

Blanche blinked. Toby, too, was wearing a new coat; when her eyes travelled across the family, she saw that all of them were wearing something. For a terrifying moment, she thought May had given them some of the clothes she'd mended for Mrs. Watson. But no. Mrs. Watson's clothing was finer than this. These clothes were warm and solid, but covered in patches, the stitches large and hurried.

"Let me see you new coat, Toby," she said, forcing her voice to be calmer.

Toby moved nearer, and Blanche crouched down, running a hand down the seams of the sleeves. The stitches were clumsy in places, and she could tell that there were asymmetries here and there from the way the coat pulled across his shoulders. But still... it was a coat, warm and serviceable.

"Like I said," said Mrs. Jackson. "She's a special one." She grasped Toby's hand firmly. "Come on, Toby. It's time to go."

Blanche watched them walk out of the tenement, speechless. She tried to ignore the part of her that burned with sorrow for this family that now had to face the streets and the oncoming winter without so much as a roof to shelter them.

Instead, she focused on what May had just done, and what it could mean for them.

When she pushed the curtain aside, May was sitting quietly at her sewing desk, working on a stuffed animal. A fox, Blanche saw, and had to crush a twinge of sadness.

"Hello, darling," she said.

May looked up at her, her smile flickering. Blanche's heart squeezed at the sight of her little girl's face. She was pale, her eyes ringed with black and purple; she'd been crying more than sleeping at night since Taylor had left.

"Hello, Mama," she said, her voice wispy with tears. "I'm almost finished."

Blanche went over to her and crouched down by the makeshift seat. "May, honey, did you make coats for the Jacksons?"

May dropped her eyes, focusing on her toy fox again. "I only used a few rags, Mama. We have enough to make animals. I'll make pretty ones and sell them for thruppence. It won't matter."

"I'm not angry, darling." Blanche put a hand on May's shoulder. "I just want you to tell me if you made those coats."

"Yes," said May faintly. Her eyes sparkled with tears again. "I didn't want them to be cold."

Blanche pulled her daughter into her arms and held her tightly, her heart throbbing for her. But at the same time, her mind was turning, considering.

Perhaps there was another way to get themselves out of this life of dreadful poverty.

***

BLANCHE'S HEART was in her mouth as they walked up to the back of yet another slop-shop. She kept a firm grip on May's hand; a dress was draped over her free arm. It was a small dress, a child's dress, but Blanche could hardly believe how beautifully it had been made. The fabric was simple – it had still cost every cent Blanche had left – but there were neat little pleats, a prettily shaped neckline, and strong hems. It was good enough to wear.

It was good enough to sell, but not for the prices that people wanted to pay street vendors. This was good enough to be sold in a shop.

"I'm tired, Mama," said May. She raised her sad blue eyes to Blanche's face. "Do you think these people will give me a job?"

"I hope so, darling," said Blanche, because if not, they had wasted an entire day and a significant amount of money on this idea and this dress. Money they didn't have, if they wanted to pay rent by the end of this week.

She knocked on the door, holding her breath and squeezing May's hand. Footsteps clumped toward them, and the door swung open to reveal a reedy young man with wide, reddened eyes.

"What do you want?" he asked brusquely.

"Sir, I'd like to offer our services to your shop," said Blanche, holding up the dress. "Here's a sample of our work."

The young man regarded them for a second, which was an improvement on the previous places they'd been to. Most people had simply slammed the door in their faces. Blanche ached every time this happened. Life had been a closed door to her for her entire life, but she'd prayed it would never have had to happen to May.

"We are hiring," he sniffed, taking the dress. He turned it this way and that, his eyes narrowing as he examined the sleeves, the skirt, the bodice. Then he turned back to Blanche. "This isn't bad. When can you start?"

"Thank you, sir," said May brightly, a real smile coming to her face. "I'm glad you like it. I worked on it all night."

The young man stared down at her. "*You?*" He turned to Blanche. "The girl made this?"

"Yes, sir. She's very talented," said Blanche bravely.

The young man snorted, shaking his head. "I've no time for liars." He tossed the dress back at Blanche.

"She's not lying, sir," cried May. "I made that with my own hands, I did."

"You're a child," he spat. "You can't make such things. Go away."

And the door slammed, again, and May stepped back, her eyes filling with tears. "Mama, why did he say that?"

"People just don't expect you to be as good at this as you are, darling," said Blanche tiredly. Dusk was settling down over the city; shops were closing, and she knew she had failed. "Come on. It's time to go home."

As they walked, she thought again of the way the young man had looked at the dress. There had been approval there. He might have hired them, she thought, if May hadn't said anything.

If he'd thought Blanche had made the dress.

An idea began to take root in her mind. There were many obstacles to it, but Blanche had scaled higher mountains in her quest to give May the life she deserved.

※

Blanche had told May she was out to fetch some more mending from Mrs. Watson, which was only partially untrue. Mrs. Watson might have something for them, after all – Blanche could only hope so, considering they had not a penny left, and there was no money for food tonight. May had cried herself to sleep from hunger as well as grief last night.

Blanche's stomach, too, felt like it was being gnawed apart from the inside out. But hunger was an old companion, one she was easy with. It was the grief in May's eyes she couldn't bear. With Taylor gone, the burden fell to Blanche alone to make everything better, and she was determined to do it.

In the cool morning light, her footsteps carried her briskly to the clothing shops on the other side of the Old Nichol, where no one would recognize her. At least, she hoped no one would recognize her. Keeping the dress draped carefully over her arm, she walked up to the first slop-shop she saw. It was not yet open; she could see an assistant sweeping the floor, and behind the counter, a chubby man peering down at a ledger through his half-moon glasses.

Blanche took a deep breath and knocked at the door. The assistant gestured angrily at her, mouthing, "We're closed."

It wasn't a good start, but Blanche couldn't let this door, too, be slammed in her face. She had to do something. Holding up the dress, she pointed at it and made a sewing motion with one hand.

The assistant looked even more annoyed. Leaving the broom, he moved between the rows of suits on hangers and shoved open the door.

"We're closed, you stupid woman," he barked.

"Sir, I'm not here to buy. I'm here to offer my services," said Blanche quickly, holding up the dress like a shield.

"Who is it, Alfred?" shouted the owner from behind the counter.

The assistant, or perhaps he might have been a son, sighed, rolling his eyes. "It's just a woman looking for work."

"Well, that other old lady died of consumption last month, so you might as well look at her work," returned the owner.

Blanche felt a chill creep down her spine at the carelessness with which the man spoke of the old woman's death. Still, she kept her smile glued in place. Alfred snatched the dress from her; the owner was moving toward them, too.

Turning the dress this way and that, Alfred gave a begrudging grunt. "The work is all right."

The owner had reached them; he took the dress from Alfred, turned it inside out and examined the seams. "A little clumsy, but it'll do," he said brusquely. He turned to Blanche. "Can you work fast?"

"This took half a day, sir," said Blanche, "and I know, with time, it'll go faster."

The owner nodded. "It'll do," he said again. "The slopworkers' quarters are on Penny Street. You'll have thirteen shillings a week, minus room and board, and light, and – "

This was going to be the difficult part. Blanche took a deep breath. "Sir, I must work from home," she said. "I have a sick father to tend to." The lie came easily; she'd told worse ones, for May's sake.

The owner and Alfred exchanged a glance. "Well, then it's no use," said Alfred sharply. "Go home and care for your father."

"Please, sir, don't send me away." It took all of her courage, but Blanche stepped over the threshold, coming within a foot of the two men. "Please, I just need a chance. I'll work harder than any of your workers, I promise. And if you don't like my work, you can always let me go. Just give me a chance."

The owner was stroking his fluffy white beard. "The work *is* good," he said begrudgingly. "But don't think that you can slight me by living in your own tenement, woman. You'll have eight shillings a week to take home, just the same as any other slop-worker."

Blanche's heart shuddered within her. Eight shillings. It was a pittance, but it would keep them alive. It would pay the rent.

They would be able to eat every day again, and perhaps there would still be time for a little mending or a few stuffed animals to be sold on the side.

It would do.

"Thank you, sir," she breathed. "Thank you."

"Alfred, bring her a list of orders," commanded the owner. "Don't waste time now." He glared at Blanche. "I expect good work from you, woman, or you can forget it."

"Always, sir. It'll be excellent work, sir," said Blanche quickly. In her heart, she could only pray that poor little May would be able to keep it up.

CHAPTER 11

M₄Y SET DOWN HER NEEDLE, rubbing her thin knuckles into her exhausted eyes. "I think it's done, Mama," she said. "See what you think."

Mama had been boiling potatoes over the fire. She came over to May, looking over her shoulder at the sewing desk and the finished ladies' coat spread out on it.

"It's absolutely wonderful, darling." she said, her voice filled with enthusiasm. "You're getting better and better at this."

May smiled. "Thank you, Mama."

Mama ran a hand over her head. "How are you liking the work, darling? I know it's only been a month, but you're getting so good at it now. I'm sure it won't be long before you get paid a little more."

"It's good work," said May, at length. She didn't want to tell Mama the truth: that she would a thousand times over rather be making the tiny animals she'd loved than these stuffy old clothes that were always the same thing over and over. Even the mending had been a little more interesting than this.

But she couldn't say that to Mama, not now that there was colour in her cheeks and food on their table every night. May knew she had to do this, and she wouldn't complain about it. Still, Mama seemed to know. She touched May's cheek, her eyes filling with sorrow again.

"Would you like to make some animals now?" she said. "You have plenty of rags left over."

May glanced at them where she'd piled them neatly on a corner of her desk. There were a few enticing scraps of green that would make the prettiest eyes for a stuffed cat. Still...

"My eyes are tired, Mama," she said. "Can I go look for Taylor, please?"

Mama's face fell. "May..."

"He's out there, Mama, I know it," said May passionately. "Please. I miss him so much – don't you?"

Mama's eyes filled suddenly and frighteningly with tears. She turned away, her voice tight. "Of course, I do."

"Then let me look for him, Mama. Please. Just until sunset. You can get the clothes ready to be taken to the shop. I'll be back before you know it. I just want to look for him for a few minutes. Please, Mama. I'll take the cow I made yesterday and try to sell it."

Mama sighed, her shoulders sagging. "All right, then," she said. "But be back by sunset, May. All right?"

"Yes, Mama." May kissed her cheek. "I love you."

Mama hugged her then, even more tightly than normal, her body trembling. "I love you, darling."

The streets were busy when May reached the bottom of the building and headed out into them. She clutched the cow under her arm, keeping her eyes on the crowd. She was looking for more than just a likely-looking customer: every boy she saw, she ran her eyes over his face, searching for that soft expression that belonged only to Taylor.

He had to be somewhere in this vast city. She turned left at the end of the street, moving toward the workhouse where she'd first seen him, starving in his pathetic coat. Was his coat still warm? Who would mend it for him if it tore?

Her heart throbbed for him. "Oh, Taylor," she whispered, her eyes searching, searching. "Where are you?"

Part of her was sure she'd find him at the end of that alley by the workhouse. Her hopeful feet took her there; as she walked, she pressed her free hand into her coat pocket, feeling for the new fox she'd made for him. She touched its pointy nose, its bushy tail. She'd win him over again with the fox, the way she'd done with the very first one.

But when May reached the end of the alley, the workhouse wall with its iron spikes rose up in front of her, tall and impenetrable. And the alley was completely empty.

Winter was upon them. Blanche shivered, pulling her warm hat down over her ears as she walked across the marketplace, her coins clutched tightly in her hand. She'd learned the hard way that walking across this particular square with one's money in one's pocket was a foolish thing to do. Even with the money in her hand, she kept a sharp eye out for pickpockets as she crossed the square.

She didn't come here often, but the smell of fried fish and chips was drawing her in. It was May's favorite, and even if it was more expensive, May had succeeded in selling that stuffed cow last night. Blanche felt she could at least give the poor little girl something of a treat tonight.

Pushing through the crowded square, Blanche tried not to think too much about last night, but her mind kept taking her back to the brokenness in May's eyes as she'd sat in front of the fire, sobbing her heart out. "I really thought he'd be there, Mama," she'd choked out. "I really hoped I would find him."

A chill gust of wind caught the edge of Blanche's skirt, sending a prickle of cold across her legs. She shuddered at the thought of Taylor, out on the streets in this. At least, she hoped he was out on the streets in this.

She thought of the blackness of that water by the docks. Of the sorrow in Taylor's eyes the last few days she'd seen him. Her heart burned with agony, and there was little she could do to stop it. She had to raise a sleeve to her eyes and dab away her tears.

"Hello?" said an annoyed voice. "Can I help you?"

Blanche realized she'd reached the front of the line at the fish-and-chip stall. "One fish, please," she mumbled, swallowing her tears. "And some chips."

The man grunted, turning to the fire behind him where a large pan of oil shimmered with heat. He pulled an old newspaper from a stack lying on the table and began to wrap up her fish in it.

A word on the front page caught her eye. *Turner.*

Blinking, she leaned closer, her heart paining yet again. It had been a long time since she'd thought of Ludwig. Her desperate affection for him seemed pitiful in the face of the way she felt about May. She didn't see him in May's big blue eyes; she thought of May when she was reminded of Ludwig. Still, she was curious to read the headline.

TURNER WIDOW MARRIES JAMES ELTON OF TRADE FORTUNE.

Disgusted, Blanche looked away. Mrs. Turner had been unbelievably wealthy, even in the wake of Ludwig's death. Now she was probably even wealthier.

And all while Ludwig's daughter was working from sunup to sundown, piecing together clothing in a drafty tenement, considering some dry fish and chips to be a special treat.

She took the offered parcel and walked back to the tenement, aching in every bone of her body. She had failed May in so many ways. If only she could get work to help bring in money. But there was no work. None at all. And she knew her tasks of washing and boiling the filthy fabric pieces, taking in mending when it was available, and in general trying to keep things going with food on the table was all she could manage. She was old before her time; life was crushing her, but she couldn't give in. She couldn't give up.

There was May.

PART IV

CHAPTER 12

Four Years Later

"What is this?" Alfred demanded, grasping the shirt by the shoulders so that it unfolded and hung in the air between them.

Blanche's toes curled. She'd thought she'd checked over all of May's work, but clearly, this one had slipped between the cracks. Clutching the bundle of fabric close to her chest, she stared at the shirt.

"It's – a shirt, sir," she managed.

"I can see that," Alfred barked. "I'm talking about *this*."

Personally, Blanche thought that the shirt was far better than anything else hanging in the slop-shop. The clothes here were as bland and unimaginative as the poor desperate souls that made them, for the most part. Even when it came down solely to function, the shirt Alfred was holding would do its part perfectly; every seam was sturdy, every measurement perfect. She knew it wasn't the quality of the work that Alfred was upset about.

It was the frills.

They were large and flowing, creamy white like the rest of the shirt, and extravagantly adorned the front of it. Blanche gritted her teeth as she gave Alfred a simpering smile, feeling a tide of love and anger toward her daughter at the same time.

"I thought they would make the shirt worth a bit more, sir," she said. "I thought they'd sell quite well, you see."

"Worth more. Woman, I gave you an order," Alfred yelled at her. "I can't sell this." He flung it at her; she was only just able to catch it before it fell into the gutter. "Fix it, and you'll have half-a-crown off your wages for the week, too."

Half-a-crown. It was a painful sum of money. "Oh, sir, please, I'll bring it back this very afternoon," she pleaded. "Don't dock the money – I'll make it up to you. I promise."

"You promised to do good work when my poor late father hired you four years ago," barked Alfred. "I suggest you make good on that promise and take what you're given."

Arguing would be useless, even dangerous. Blanche stepped back, tucking the shirt into the bundle of new fabric she'd been given. "Yes, sir. I'm terribly sorry, sir."

"Bring that shirt back this afternoon, or you'll face the consequences," Alfred barked.

He slammed the door then, and Blanche closed her eyes so that she wouldn't have to see it close in her face as so many other doors had done.

The worst part, right now, was that she felt she had to do the same thing to May when she got home.

MAY STARED DOWN DISTASTEFULLY at the freshly cut fabric on her desk. Green. She was so tired of this same shade of boring brownish green that the slop-shop was forever sending to her. And the fact that she always had to make it into the same cut of boring trousers was certainly not helping matters.

She sighed, propping her chin on her hands. She knew what she had to do, of course. Pick up her needle, thread it, and then put these pieces together the way she'd done a thousand times before, to make yet another pair of those trousers that the slop-shop's customers seemed to like so much. It was easy work, but her heart groaned to do something different, something more fun.

Reaching into the basket of scraps by her side, she took out a piece of bright red. It had been such a long time since she'd made something she liked. With longing, she thought of the sweet little stuffed animals she'd always made, until the slop-shop had increased her workload – and her wages. Mama said there was no more need of those animals and that it was much safer for May to be up here in the tenement rather than selling them on the street.

So she made slop-shop clothes, and it felt as though her heart was shrivelling up within her from the boredom of it.

Holding up the piece of red fabric, she turned it this way and that against the green. A pocket, perhaps? A little detailing along the stitching? Maybe just the inside of a pocket, so that when one reached in to pull out one's watch, a flash of bright red would be seen.

There were footsteps on the stairs, and May quickly shoved the red into her basket, jumping to her feet. Moments later, Mama pushed the curtain aside and stepped into the room. "Hello, darling," she said.

"Mama." May wrapped her arms around her mother, startled as always by how small Mama had become in her embrace. It wasn't so long ago that Mama had seemed towering and invincible. Now, she was a frail creature in May's arms; when they both straightened, May realized with a jolt that she had to look down into her mother's eyes.

"Have you been all right up here?" Mama asked, touching May's cheek.

"Yes, Mama, I've been fine. I'm just about to start sewing these trousers." May gestured to them. "How was your walk?"

"Cold," Mama admitted. "Winter is coming." She set down a bundle of fabric on the desk and handed May the handwritten slip of orders for the week. May took it eagerly, her eye darting down the lines to see what she would have to make. Her heart sank in dismay.

"Oh, Mama, *more* of those trousers?" she said. "They're so dull."

"I'm afraid slop-shop clothing isn't exactly exciting, my love," said Mama. "It's what sells, so that's what they order."

"I know." May sighed, dreading the thought of having to sew another pair of these trousers every single day for the next week. Even Sunday; otherwise she would never make these orders. "I just wish I could make something a little more interesting."

"I see you *have* made something a little more interesting, darling." Mama frowned, disappointment in her eyes.

"Oh." May's hands fell to her sides. "Didn't they like the frills?"

"What did you expect, May?" said Mama, her voice bubbling with frustration. "It wasn't what they'd ordered."

"I thought they'd like it, Mama. I thought they'd see, if they let me make my ideas, people would buy them."

"No one is going to buy a frilly shirt from a slop-shop, darling." Mama threw up her hands. "At any rate, they sent it back. You're to change it by this afternoon, and they docked half-a-crown from our wages for the week, too."

"Half-a-crown." A tide of sadness ran through May. "Mama, I'm so sorry. I didn't mean for it to hurt you." Her eyes stung with tears. "I... I just wanted to make something beautiful."

"I know, darling." Mama sank into their only chair, leaning her head back against the wall, exhausted.

"It hurts my heart that they're punishing me for making something special." May folded her arms.

"Sweetheart, I know. But we have to do what the slop-shop wants. Please, darling." Mama's eyes grew desperate. "Please don't make this harder than it already is."

May felt a pang of guilt. She went over to her mother, wrapping her in another hug. "I'm so sorry, Mama. I didn't mean to make trouble for you."

Mama sighed, returning the embrace. "I know you didn't."

May leaned her head on Mama's shoulder, wondering what those men at the slop-shop had said to her. They could be terribly cruel, she knew, and she was the one who had caused them to be cruel to Mama.

It was just so hard not to make things beautiful as well as functional. She would have to come up with another way to allow the desire for beauty within her to find its outlet.

※

A DEAFENING SCREAM woke Taylor from his bed in the hayloft. He kept his eyes closed, wishing he could have just five more minutes; but the squealing sound came again, followed by a massive crash of iron on iron.

"Pollywog, stop it," he moaned, rolling over on the hay and drawing his fists up under his chin to warm them. Even with the heat of the horses rising up through the wooden floor, and the soft cushion of the hay that formed his bed, the loft was cold. There was a thin draft blowing in under the eaves that chilled his bones.

The pony gave another bad-tempered squeal and kicked the stable door again. If he made much more noise, he'd be sure to wake old Mr. Hayes, the stable master – and then there would be nothing but trouble. Yawning, Taylor dragged himself to his feet. He picked bits of hay from his hair and clothes as he stumbled down the stairs and into the stables below.

A cacophony of equine noises greeted him when he reached the aisle. It was a low, narrow shed, filled with a rich farmer's collection of horses: towering drafts for the farm work, pretty hackneys for the carriage, saddle horses, and Pollywog, the demonic pony that the farmer kept for his children. This latter was busy chomping on the wood of its stable door, its eyes wild.

"I'm coming, I'm coming," said Taylor, grasping a bucket. The back-breaking work of watering came first. It was the first thing the old stable master had taught him – *always water before feeding* – just one of the many iron-clad rules that seemed to Taylor that they had been pounded into his bones.

It had been two years ago, on a morning even colder than this, that Taylor had come to this stable for the very first time. He remembered that morning as he began to work the pump, sending cold water seething into the bucket. On that morning, the air had been so cold that it had felt like needles entering Taylor's lungs.

He wasn't sure how he'd survived that night before he'd first come here, his last night in London. It had seemed as though every surface in the world was frozen or frosted over. The pavement had been treacherous to his feet; the mud in the slums even worse, pock-marked with footprints, frozen into perilous divots and ditches that had snagged at his painful feet. He'd already lost all but his two big toes to frostbite by then, and his feet were ragged and bleeding as he stumbled this way and that, searching desperately for even an unoccupied doorway to get out of the wind. But sparkling icicles hung from every surface, making everywhere seem impassable. Taylor knew that to stop moving would be death. So he carried on, pushing through the cold wind, walking though he felt he had no strength. He hadn't eaten in days.

It had been well past midnight when he saw the train: a sleek creature, dusted by frost, yet nonetheless waiting on the tracks, its nose pointing to somewhere else. Taylor had no idea what lay beyond London. The world, he supposed, where all of May's lions and tigers came from.

The thought of May made his heart sting. He reached into his pocket, touching the frayed little fox she'd given him on that first night. It had been two years, then, since he'd last seen her. There had been so many times he had wanted to go back. Now, he knew that going back would mean his survival... but at what cost? May was happier without him. They must have moved to a better tenement by now. Perhaps she even had real meat to eat every single day. The thought made a hot tear run down his frozen cheek. May deserved every droplet of the happiness she had found.

And if that meant the end of Taylor, then so be it.

The train station was quiet and very empty. Taylor moved through it, looking for somewhere to lie down. Under a bench, perhaps, although he'd still be exposed to the howling wind. Then, he heard a flapping. A rustling. A canvas covering had come loose from one of the cars, and was snapping in the wind, a rope dangling from it. It had been covering up a series of boxes stacked on the train, and there was an inviting little hollow among the boxes, one that would neatly shelter an emaciated boy.

Taylor had seen only a warm place to huddle for a few hours, and he'd scrambled up into it, pulled the canvas down over himself, and made it fast. Then, out of the wind for the first time in days, he'd slept and slept. When he woke, the train was in a whole new world. He'd scrambled out from under his covering into a place with long fields bordered by stone walls, all asleep under a blanket of snow.

It had been almost by chance that he'd stumbled upon the stables. He'd been going from place to place, asking for work as he always did. And it was old Mr. Hayes who had finally taken pity on him. His stable lad had gone off to get married, and he'd needed a new one.

That was two years ago. Now, Taylor had finished watering every horse, and he turned to make his way to the feed room. He started to scoop oats and chaff into the waiting buckets. In a few minutes he was tipping buckets into the mangers, dodging a bad-tempered bite from Pollywog, and then the stable was filled with the peaceful sound of horses chewing.

Taylor stood at the end of the aisle for a moment. and despite the hunger that pinched at his stomach, and the exhaustion that nipped at the corners of his eyes, he felt a bubble of contentment rising in his heart. The work was brutal, and he had little in the way of wages. Room and board – and two shillings a week.

But the peace in this place, surrounded by horses, was something he hadn't known since the last time he'd looked into May Eplett's eyes.

CHAPTER 13

Mama was asleep. May could tell by the deep slowness of her breathing, and the heaviness of her arm where it was draped over May's ribs. She took Mama's hand very carefully, moving it out of the way, and rolled off the sleeping pallet to sneak across the room.

Lighting a candle would wake Mama, and besides, candles were so expensive. May wouldn't waste one on something like this. But it was a clear night, and in the square of moonlight drifting in from the window, she couldn't resist reaching for her basket of scraps and her needle and thread.

The idea had come to her just as she was beginning to fall asleep. She pulled out a few chunks of fabric: mustard yellow, deep auburn. Twisting them together, she held them up to the moonlight, cocking her head this way and that. She added a tiny strip of bright blue, then began to cut, the picture dazzlingly clear in her mind.

The image in her mind had lace and feathers in it, and silk, and ribbons. Just like she'd seen on the ladies that passed her on the street back when she was still allowed to go outside and sell her toys. She didn't have any of those things now, but at least she could imitate what she'd imagined.

The moonlight began to fade as she sewed, cobbling together the idea in quick, clumsy movements before it could be torn away from her. In the last sliver of light, she held it up. A hat, the auburn colour just complementing the mustard, a tiny strip of blue representing the peacock feather she'd imagined in its place. The sight of it called a deep sigh from within her heart. She could have made something splendid now, if only she'd been allowed to, if only she'd had what she needed.

She closed her eyes, smiling as she imagined what Taylor would say. *May, it's so lovely.* He didn't know the first thing about what was beautiful when it came to clothes, but he'd have been impressed just because she was the one who'd made it. Her heart stung. She missed him so.

Quietly, she tucked the hat away in her basket and curled back up on the pallet beside Mama. She was exhausted, her eyes and fingers cramping, but sleep just wouldn't come to her. Ideas danced across her mind when she closed her eyes. The hat could have a coat that went with it, something long and elegant that flared over the skirts, mustard yellow with that glimpse of auburn on the inside...

May sighed, pillowing her head on her arm, and tried to find a more comfortable position on the hard pallet. Someday, she might be able to pour herself into making beautiful things. And if someone would finally see the beauty in her work, then perhaps she could sell those things for much more money. She could open her own millinery, and people would come from everywhere to wear her beautiful clothes.

And they'd have a safe, warm home, and plenty of food. She shifted a little closer to Mama, listening to her mother's deep, slow breaths. That dream felt like it was a very, very long way away. But she would cling to it, and hope that someday, she and Mama would both have a better future.

THE OLD GREY gelding was looking a little better. He towered over Taylor, a huge, impassive wall of horseflesh, motionless where he stood on the soft grassy knoll right behind the back garden of the manor house. Taylor had been nursing the old horse's bellyache all day, and now at last, the gelding was standing quietly.

Taylor patted the huge swell of the creature's neck, feeling his knees and feet cramp with exhaustion. It had been a long day of walking him up and down, pausing to drench him with salt, holding him while the horse doctor shoved gigantic horse-balls of medicine down his throat. Now, at last, the gelding seemed better. Mr. Hayes had told him to take him out to graze on the soft green grass, but so far, he didn't seem interested.

"Come on, Badger, old chap," said Taylor, reaching up to scratch him at the base of the mane where he liked it. "Just a few bites."

A rich country evening was descending on the manor grounds, painting their surroundings in gold. The back garden lay still and cold; nothing was growing now, not so late in the autumn. The only colour belonged to the clothes snapping on the washing-line. As Taylor waited, keeping an eye on the watchful old horse, a maid came out of the scullery and headed over to the washing-line with a basket on her hip.

"Hello there," she called out, waving.

Taylor felt heat creeping unbidden across his cheeks. It was always that way when one of the maids saw him. She was pretty, too, with a dark wing of hair falling over her eyes, and strong curves that moved gracefully as she took a sheet down from the line.

It made something flutter right behind Taylor's belly button. He turned away to look back at old Badger, who was cropping the grass in hungry mouthfuls.

"Your name is Taylor, isn't it?" the maid persisted. "I'm Susie."

Taylor cleared his throat twice before he could speak. "Y-yes, it is."

She laughed. It was a tinkling sound, but it made no fun of him, and for that reason Taylor looked up at her and dared a smile. She tossed that wonderful dark hair as she pulled another piece of linen down from the line. "What's the matter with the horse? I saw the doctor came out to see him."

"Oh, it was colic. But he's all right now." Taylor beamed, giving the horse's shoulder a friendly slap. "It'll take more than a bit of bellyache to get Badger down for long."

"Badger. That's a sweet name. Strange name for a white horse, though."

"He's not white – he's grey," said Taylor eagerly. "Even horses that *look* white are born a dark colour, and slowly turn more and more grey as they get older." The knowledge simply spilled out of him in his excitement.

Susie didn't seem to mind. She listened intently, nodding along as though this truly interested her, and Taylor found himself taking a step nearer, tugging old Badger over to the fence so that it was easier to talk with her. "Where are you from?" he asked. "You sound different."

"Yorkshire," said Susie. "And you sound just as different."

"I'm from London."

"London?" She shook her head. "I've heard that's a hard, hard place."

Dark memories crossed Taylor's mind like shadows. He took a deep breath, trying to hold back the nervousness that threatened to swamp him just at the thought of his time in the city. "It... it is," he managed at length. "But I'm here now."

"So, you are." Susie smiled at him then, and she had the most beautiful deep dimples on either cheek, sweetly symmetrical, exactly like May's. Until that moment, Taylor had almost forgotten that small detail of May's pretty face, and suddenly he felt like a traitor. He stepped back, tightening his grip on Badger's rope.

Susie hadn't noticed the qualm of horror shuddering through Taylor's soul. "Some of us girls are going down to the fair in the town square on Sunday afternoon, when we have our time off. Why don't you come with us?"

"I – I don't think I can." Taylor dragged Badger's head up from the grass. "I'm sorry." He felt an overwhelming urge to get away, to stop smiling into this girl's lovely face. Suddenly she didn't seem as pretty anymore. Not in comparison with his memories of May.

She blinked at him. "Oh... all right. Another time, then."

Taylor made no response. He turned and walked briskly back in the direction of the stable, feeling a jagged crack of longing run through his heart.

THE STITCHES TRICKLED AUTOMATICALLY through May's fingers. She had made so many of these same ladies' coats to this same pattern that she believed she could do it in her sleep by now; and indeed, she felt as though she was sleeping, her brain dormant, her hands working of their own accord.

It was hateful.

She tried humming to herself as she threaded the needle again, cut the thread and went on working. But she only knew a handful of songs. She'd learned most of them from the tiny church near their tenement; she could hear the tunes of the hymns of a Sunday morning as she worked, if not most of the words. So she made her own words, and sang them quietly to herself as she worked.

As she sang her way through something about a shepherd – she had made it into a little ballad about a lonely shepherd boy – she heard the church bell strike noon and had to stifle a groan. Mama was still out looking for the cheapest coal to buy, and she would still be working until sunset. It felt like she'd been at this for a terribly long time and the hours of drudgery stretched out before her with no promise of variety or excitement.

It was at times like these that her mind wandered all too easily. Wandered back to Taylor. Her heart stung at the thought of him. Just yesterday, she had begged Mama to allow her to go out just across the street to buy some bread. The journey had taken all of fifteen minutes in total, but for every one of those minutes, she'd kept her eyes peeled for him. She'd even called his name a few times, as though he was hiding somewhere nearby, close enough to hear her.

But Taylor didn't come. It had been four years, and still he didn't come.

She let out a long sigh, setting down the half-made coat and shaking a dreadful cramp out of her fingers. Getting to her feet, she went over to the tiny window and peered out at the gray street. A soft drizzle was falling. Below her, umbrellas moved anonymously, little spots of prosperity among holey hats and bent, bowed heads.

May felt, rather than heard, the burst of excitement rush through the tenement building. She had lived in this place for long enough – since she could remember – that she knew all of its moods and felt the ripple of emotion rising through the floors, a rustle of conversation starting and growing until it reached the tenement next door. There had been several neighbours over the years to replace the Jacksons, and the latest was a young couple, Molly and Pete. May heard Molly gasp, then Pete's footsteps rush across the floor.

Although she knew she shouldn't, since Mama had always told her to stay quietly in the tenement if there was ever a disturbance in the building, May hurried over to the curtain and pulled it aside just a crack. The door was open; she just saw

Pete disappearing down the hall. Molly, pale and wide-eyed, was standing beside it, her hand over her mouth.

"Molly?" May asked nervously. "What's happening?"

Molly turned to her, her pale eyes wide. "Oh, May, it's just too dreadful." she cried, clapped her hands over her face and flung herself upon her pallet, sobbing.

May knew Molly well enough to be sure she wouldn't get a coherent word out of her now. She would have to see for herself. Grabbing her coat, she pulled it snugly over her shoulders and hurried out of the tenement and down the hallway.

At first, she went cautiously, wondering if a fight had broken out among the tenants – it wouldn't be the first time. But by the time she reached the ground floor, she could tell that whatever the trouble was, the tenants' voices were raised in fear, not anger. A crowd had gathered around the front door; Pete was among them, and his face was ashen.

"Pete?" May called to him. "What is it?"

He turned, pointing at the door. A piece of paper had been nailed to it, with words painted across it in an angry splash of red.

"What does it say?" May cried. She'd never learned to read.

An old gentleman, bent double over his walking stick, was peering worriedly at the sign through a cracked monocle.

Largely illiterate, the rest of the tenants waited in a sudden hush to hear what he had to say.

"It says," he said, his voice wobbling, "that the building has been condemned."

A gasp ran through the crowd, and everyone started talking at once. May couldn't make out what any of it meant. "What does that mean?" she cried. "What does 'condemned' mean?"

"May." Mama's voice cut through the crowd. So did she, shoving people aside, her hands clutching a bag of coal as she reached May. She tossed the coal onto her shoulder and seized May's arm. "What are you doing down here?"

"Something's happened, Mama," said May. "What does 'condemned' mean?"

"I told you never to come down here when there was a fuss like this," said Mama angrily. She began to tow May away from the door.

"What's happening, Mama?" May twisted her neck around to glance back at the crowd as Mama pulled her up the first flight of stairs.

"Don't you worry about it, May. Just go back inside and do your work where you're safe."

"But I don't understand. Everyone seems so afraid. Why are they so scared if there's nothing to worry about?"

They'd reached an empty hallway, and Mama turned to her, her eyes glittering with exasperation. When they met May's, they softened. She reached up, cupping May's face in one tired, hard hand.

"I forget how grown up you're becoming, my darling," she said softly.

"I just want to know what it means. Please, Mama." May swallowed. "I'm scared."

Mama passed a hand over her face, letting out a shuddering sigh.

"What does it mean that the building's been condemned?" May asked.

"It means that it's not safe for us to live in it anymore, darling." Mama shook her head. "It's probably been unsafe ever since we moved here, but now some big-wig has noticed, and they're going to tear it down."

"Tear it down." May gasped. "But where will we go?"

Mama turned her face away, so that May couldn't look into her eyes when she responded. But she heard the fear trembling in her voice.

"I don't know, my love. I just don't know."

CHAPTER 14

Taylor saw trouble coming before the pony's rider did. It was a sharply pretty pony, with a tidy, chiselled face and small erect ears that poked out from a luxurious torrent of forelock; a flashy, copper-coloured chestnut with four white legs, it trotted down the road with its tail high and every sign of fieriness in the strong lines of its short body.

There was nothing wrong with the pony, Taylor assessed, walking along the verge of the road toward town. But disaster was imminent. That much was evident from the way its rider, a portly boy carrying a riding crop in one hand, was clenching the reins in a chubby fist as though he had some kind of mastery over the little animal. Any horseman knew that one never had mastery over a pony, especially not a chestnut mare like this one, with a wall-eye and big nostrils that flared with spirit. And anyway, even if one could be so firm as to bodily control a chestnut pony mare, it wouldn't be this boy. His backside slapped gracelessly on the saddle with every stride; the stirrups clanged loosely on his feet.

Shaking his head, Taylor went on his way with half an eye on pony and rider. It seemed bitterly unfair that this boy, with his rough hand and arrogant face, should be trotting to town on such a fine and pretty pony when he clearly had no respect for it. From his soft white hands and the fine, crisp clothes he wore, Taylor was certain this boy had never so much as saddled his own pony before, let alone mucked out a stable. But he was the one riding while Taylor had to walk forty-five minutes into town just for a change of scenery on his Sunday afternoon off. By the time he'd gone to town and back, he barely had two hours to spare for anything else.

If he only had a pony like that, Taylor thought, he'd ride to London in a matter of hours. He knew Mr. Hayes would give him one day off from work; he was a good old soul really, and Taylor had never let him down. If he had a pony, one day would be enough to ride to London and find that tenement once more. He could find May. He could tell her that he had work now, that he mattered. He would find his way easily, he knew it, and then he could look into her blue eyes again.

And see if she really was as beautiful in real life as she was in his memories.

The pony saw the partridge in the hedge long before even Taylor did. She had passed him at a brisk trot when her ears suddenly pricked up sharply. The nostrils flared, and there was a moment's hesitation of her hooves on the road. The boy didn't notice; he just bumped away on the saddle, oblivious. As they grew nearer, the pony's stride shortened still more, but it was only when she slowed right down that the boy realized something was happening.

Taylor knew that a single word of encouragement from the right rider would have sent that pony on without batting an eye. But as the partridge began to flutter and cluck nervously in the hedge, the boy reached back with his riding crop and landed a loud blow squarely upon the loins of the pony. Many a pony would have taken the blow without protest, but not this one. She didn't bother to leap or rear at all. She simply dropped her shoulder in a practiced little twisting movement, and the boy was deposited onto the road before he knew what was happening.

The boy set up a horrible noise, but the pony seemed quite unconcerned. Snorting at the partridge – which was fluttering off into the field – she tossed up her tail and trotted away, reins and stirrups dangling.

The boy was already sitting up and Taylor couldn't see any sign of injury, so he broke into a jog after the pony, whistling softly. "Whoa, sweetheart," he called after her. "Steady on."

The pony had no intention of listening to him or anyone else. She lengthened her stride, moving off at a steady clip. Taylor's stomach tightened at the thought of the railway crossing she was approaching. He moved a little faster, reaching into his pocket to pull out the handful of oats he always kept there.

"Steady, girl," he called, shaking the oats in his hand. "Look what I've got for you."

Hearing the rustle of oats, the pony slowed to a walk, looking over her shoulder. Taylor opened his hand, and her nostrils flared, catching the scent. She came to a halt and stood quietly until he reached her, then reached out and lipped it softly out of his hand.

"There you are, beauty," said Taylor, grasping her reins. "You're all right."

With a great huffing and puffing, the boy was striding over to them, his natty jacket and jodhpurs covered in dust.

"Give me that." he barked, snatching the reins from Taylor. "You wretched animal." he yelled, jerking at the reins and brandishing his crop.

The pony leaped up onto her hind legs, flailing wildly, her eyes wide with fear, yanking the boy forward. She nearly pulled away from him, but Taylor plucked the reins out of his hands, and when the pony came down, he put a hand on her shoulder to soothe her.

"How could you treat your pony like this?" he shouted at the boy. "Don't you see you're frightening her?"

"Don't speak to me like that, boy," barked the boy.

Taylor hesitated, but all of a sudden, he remembered May, the way she'd pleaded so passionately with her mother to help the Jacksons. A surge of courage gripped him. "Well, then don't mistreat your pony. You're lucky to have a beautiful pony like this."

The boy pushed back his dishevelled hair. "It's not my pony, you dunce," he shouted. "It's a livery pony, and I shall go straight back to that idiot and demand my father's money back for hiring out this dangerous animal."

He made a grab for the reins again, and Taylor dodged him. "Where is the livery?"

"Just there." The boy gestured furiously. "Give me that pony."

The pony reared again, her small feet flailing in the air, and Taylor dodged them deftly, but the boy was less agile. A hoof gave him a sound clout on the shoulder, and he jumped back with a squeal of pain.

"I'll walk the pony," said Taylor firmly. He couldn't have been feeling less charitable toward the boy at that moment, but he couldn't let him put another finger on the pony.

The boy was clutching his shoulder, red in the face. "M-maybe you should," he said, the fight clearly gone out of him.

It was only a few hundred yards' walk further to the livery yard, which turned out to be on the very edge of town. It was a small, square yard surrounded by loose boxes; horses watched attentively over their stable doors as grooms bustled to and fro. There was a small office in the middle of the stable row on the opposite side of the yard, and the boy stormed furiously toward it.

Taylor, wide-eyed, drank it all in as he led the pony up to the office. There was a vast variety of horses standing in the stables: tall, elegant ladies' hacks; solid cobs with strong legs; fluffy little ponies with mild eyes; hunters, all rippling muscle and trembling energy.

The boy hammered on the office door. It opened, and a middle-aged man stepped out. His figure was still as firm and slender in his jodhpurs as it might have been years ago; but his left arm was held at a crooked angle, and his face was as wizened as neglected leather.

"Well?" he said, his eyes sparkling with shrewdness. "Enjoy your ride on Spark, did you?"

"That animal is dangerous, Mr. Goswick," the boy shouted, pointing angrily. "It threw me in the road, just half a mile from here, and bolted."

"That's not true, sir," Taylor cried. "There's not a dangerous thing about this pony. She's a gem, she is, I swear it. If this boy could ride, he would have had the most wonderful time with her."

"Silence, you pathetic dimwit," shouted the boy. "I am a most accomplished rider."

"Sir, please, he could hardly sit on this pony, let alone control her," retorted Taylor.

"My father will have your tongue."

"Quiet," rapped Mr. Goswick. "That's enough of that." He caught Taylor's eye. "I'm well aware that young Mr. Adams here cannot ride, which is why I originally suggested a nice, well-behaved cob for you, young sir."

"A cob," spluttered the boy. "An ugly *cob*."

"A cob which would have brought you home safely whether you could ride or not," retorted Mr. Goswick. "But you insisted on something 'finer', and so I gave you Spark here, since she specializes in bringing silly little boys down a peg."

"My father will hear about this," spat the boy.

"Your father is well aware, and condoned my plan," said Mr. Goswick smoothly. "Now, Mr. Adams, if you would kindly go home and think about your own foolish pride, perhaps you would be the better off for it."

Spluttering, the boy stormed away, waving his riding crop and blustering about his father. Mr. Goswick turned to Taylor and seemed about to say something when a young lady and gentleman walked into the yard, and he turned to them attentively. Taylor held Spark's reins, watching, as they told him they'd come up from London by train and wanted to hire a pair of horses to ride around the park. Mr. Goswick showed them a pair of beautiful hacks, then named his price for the day's hire.

Taylor almost fell over with shock at the princely sum he named. It was more than he himself made in two months' work. Taylor was no good at arithmetic, but he knew that horses didn't cost anywhere near that sum to keep.

Mr. Goswick was making a healthy profit.

The possibilities flooded his mind. He thought of how he'd wished he had a pony like Spark, and how he could ride down and visit May for a day if that was the case. But if he really did have a pony of his own – or a horse – he could hire it out and make far more money than he could ever dream of making as a stable hand. He wouldn't have to beg a day off from Mr. Hayes; he could go where he wanted and run his own life.

And make enough money, perhaps, to be more than just some desperate street urchin, some downtrodden stable boy.

Mr. Goswick had finished with his customers and glanced over at Taylor as an afterthought. "Bert, take that pony," he ordered, gesturing to one of the lads.

The boy hurried over to take Spark's reins, but Taylor clung on. "Sir. Mr. Goswick," he cried.

"Yes, yes, boy, you've done well, now go home," grumbled Mr. Goswick, opening his office door.

"Sir, please, I want to help. Please – "

"I have enough stable lads. Go home."

"No, sir, I already have work. But I have every Sunday afternoon off, sir, and if you would let me, I want to come here and help you and learn about the livery."

Mr. Goswick paused, looking at him, an eyebrow raised. "I told you, boy..."

"I don't need to be paid," said Taylor desperately. "Just let me learn."

Mr. Goswick shook his head. "Then you're a fool. Go home."

He walked away, and Taylor knew that the conversation was thoroughly over.

***

BLANCHE'S BODY ACHED. She dragged herself up the street one step at a time, her back stooped, feeling as though her knees and ankles had become solid bone. How old was she? She found herself wondering idly about this as she walked. May would be thirteen this year. How old had she been when May was born? Seventeen? Eighteen? That made her about thirty. She wondered if it was normal, at thirty, to feel like one was hundred years old, like the road of life had just been stretching on for far too long.

She passed a hand over her face, feeling its cold against her cheeks, trying to shake off the strange thought that had just crossed her mind. She couldn't think like this. She had so much work to do. May would grow up into a better life than Blanche had ever had, if Blanche died trying. It was her singular purpose, had been ever since she'd brought that baby girl into the world, and she was going to make it happen. No, she realized, she couldn't die trying. She just had to succeed, whatever the odds.

And the first step, right now, was finding them another tenement in which to live.

The panicked exodus from their building had caused every available space in a reasonable radius of their old building to fill up in a matter of days. Those spaces that were still available had become exorbitantly priced. Those eight shillings a week didn't go very far, and Blanche was growing increasingly desperate. This would be the third building she visited: the other two had both turned her away when they had learned that she was *Miss* Eplett, not married.

This place would work. It had to work, and if she had to lie to get it, then so be it. Blanche was approaching it now: a thin slip of building squashed between two others, staring down at her with gaping rectangular windows that watched her like uneasy eyes as she approached the front door.

The owner was standing in front of the building in a cheap business suit, smoking. He watched her approach, dragging down another puff of white smoke, and let it escape slowly through her nostrils as she drew nearer.

"Mr. Commons?" she said. "Did you get my note?"

Mr. Commons waited to exhale all of the smoke before responding, his eyes assessing her. "I did indeed," he said. "And I was surprised that anyone interested in this kind of accommodation would be able to write."

"Anyone can fall on hard times, sir," she said.

He watched her for a moment more, then shrugged languidly. "Let's hope not. Let me show you the rooms."

He led her into a narrow hallway that nonetheless seemed to have most of its floorboards intact. Her hopes were beginning to rise when they climbed to the very top floor on a staircase that creaked and moaned but didn't actually shudder under their feet; when they reached the top, the rooms seemed to be sectioned off with wooden walls instead of curtains.

"There's a lavatory on the ground floor," said Mr. Commons. He pushed open the door of one of the rooms, showing her a tiny, bare space that nonetheless had a small fireplace and, most crucially, a large window. Sunlight streamed into the room.

Blanche's heart trembled with hope. "Oh, this room would be perfect," she said. "I'm a slopworker, you see." The lie had become easy. "I need the light."

"I see," said Mr. Commons, leaning against the wall with his hands in his pockets. "Well, the rent is three shillings a week."

"Three shillings." Blanche's heart all but stopped. How was she meant to feed and clothe them, as well as replacing needles and thread (which the slop-shop did not supply), on such a pitiful sum?

"That's the price." Mr. Commons shrugged.

Blanche stared longingly at the big window. "Oh, sir, have you nothing cheaper?"

"Well... I suppose you could live in the cellar."

The cellar. Blanche swallowed hard. Cellars were damp and dark; she'd spent a few months in one when she'd just been evicted from Ludwig's townhouse. But what choice did she have? They were days away from being forcibly removed from the tenement. And then May would be on the street...

Anything was better than that. She drew herself up, wrestling for a semblance of dignity. "Please show me the cellar."

"All right, then," said Mr. Commons.

He led her back down the stairs, and with every step they drew further and further away from the neat, warm room with its big window, and moved down instead to a tiny cold cellar that had no light at all. Mr. Commons lit a candle and held it up, its golden glow illuminating a stone floor, a few ventilation shafts, and bare walls. There was a boiler right near the back.

"I wasn't counting on renting this place out, but if you'll take it, I'll rig up a little fireplace that shares a chimney with the boiler," he said.

It was an uncharacteristically kind offer, although Blanche knew that this unexpected profit made it more than worth it for the owner. "And what would rent be?" she asked.

"A shilling and six," said Mr. Commons promptly.

Blanche swallowed. It was a far sight better than three shillings, even though her heart quailed within her at the thought of housing beautiful May in this dinghy hole. Already, May's heart seemed to be outgrowing the bounds of their tenement. She tried to imagine her daughter sitting here, day after day, sewing away quietly by candlelight.

The thought disgusted her, but she'd done the arithmetic with the swiftness of a woman on the brink of poverty. Candles were expensive, and they'd still be much worse off than they had been at their old building, but they could make it work in the cellar. There was no choice.

She was going to put her baby girl in the cellar and lock her in darkness to work away her days.

The thought crippled her, yet somehow, she managed to pay the man, and then somehow, she was walking outside and down the street to break the news to May. Somehow, she was still going.

Somehow.

CHAPTER 15

Taylor peered through the hedge at the bustling livery yard. Even though it was noon on a Sunday, there was plenty of work being done. People were bringing back horses and carts they'd hired to drive to church far away; others were coming to hire horses for pleasure riding on such a beautifully sunny afternoon. As a result, the yard was full, and stable lads were scurrying everywhere, performing the thousand familiar little tasks that had become part of Taylor's day. Saddling up; sponging sweat from tired horses; oiling hooves; brushing out manes and tails so that each animal looked stately and beautiful as it was led out onto the yard to its rider.

He had spent all week running around after those tasks, but right now, he longed to be a part of them, and to learn everything there was to learn about the business. With an envious eye, he watched as Mr. Goswick took a sheaf of paper money from a young man in exchange for the reins of a fine black hunter. That was more money than Taylor had ever seen in his life. It was certainly more money than he had been bought for, from the orphanage.

It was enough money to change his life forever, and then he could ride to London anytime he wanted, and sweep May off her feet, and give her the world.

He closed his eyes, remembering her face, and his heart stung at the memory. May was beautiful, but it was not her beauty that had made her shine like the first rose in bloom amid a world of frost and dead leaves. It was the essence of her, the beauty of her spirit that shone from those blue eyes and bathed the world in its richness. Being near May was like stretching out one's hands to a crackling hearth fire. It was like coming in from the cold, and Taylor had been cold for so, so long.

A long sigh escaped him, and he opened his eyes with renewed determination. Whatever came, he had to find a way to buy his own horse and start running his own livery. Or even put together enough money to hire a horse from Mr. Goswick for the day. Whatever it took to be near May, that was what he would do.

There was a brief lull; all the customers had left for now, and the stable lads were busy putting horses up, throwing hay, mixing feeds. Mr. Goswick stood in front of his office, hands on his hips, watching the activity with a sharp eye. This would be Taylor's best chance. He slipped out from behind the hedge and walked purposefully into the yard, swinging his arms and doing his best not to look too nervous.

Mr. Goswick spotted him at once. The wizened goblin face creased deeply with distaste, and he raised his chin, shouting across the yard before Taylor could reach him. "What do you want, boy?"

Taylor took a deep breath. "Sir, I've come back to find out if you need any help."

Mr. Goswick shook his head. "And what makes you think something would have changed between now and last week?"

"I don't know, sir," said Taylor, "but I thought I would try."

Mr. Goswick waved an impatient hand. "I don't have time for your games, boy. Get off my yard."

Taylor had spent so much time hearing variations on that theme. *Get out of my shop. Get off my property. Go away.* A thousand angry faces came back to him, a thousand rejections raining down upon his shoulders the way they had done in London, and his heart trembled within him. He stepped back, ready to turn away and go home with his tail between his legs like he'd done so many times before, but something stopped him. It was the thought of May, and the sudden despairing hope he felt lurching in his chest, and the aching knowledge that he didn't want to be without her for a single minute longer than he had to.

Taylor turned back to the old man, summoning his courage. "Sir, please, if you ever need help…"

"I don't need help. Now clear off before I set the dogs on you," snapped Mr. Goswick.

Taylor crept out of the yard in abject misery. Yet again, he was falling short.

***

This was no home. It was a dungeon.

Frozen in dismay, May stood in the doorway, staring into the cellar that Mama had just told her was to be her new home. The faint lines of its walls and ceiling were sketched out in red from the glow of the boiler at the back of the cellar, and those shapes were all so straight, so brutal. There was nothing soft, nothing beautiful in sight, not even a shard of warm sunlight to pour into the cellar, not even a glimpse of sky to gaze at when the world was at its darkest.

A match hissed, and Mama lit a candle, holding it up. Even in the warm gold of its light, the cellar seemed like a prison. It was completely bare but for the tiny ramshackle fireplace in one corner, the sleeping pallet with their threadbare blankets and newspaper mattress, and a familiar sight: an upturned bucket and a big wooden box. May's sewing desk.

"What do you think, my love?" asked Mama.

May wished she could express her true opinion of this place: that it was a cave of misery, that it would kill her, slowly, like a small bird suffocating in an unfeeling fist. Yet when she looked into Mama's eyes, she saw terror there. How could she tell Mama she hated everything about this cellar? It was the best Mama could do.

"It's nice and warm, Mama," said May.

Mama's face relaxed a little. "It *is* warm," she said. "And look – I've bought plenty of candles."

May knew what that meant: that there wouldn't be enough money for food tonight, maybe not for tomorrow night either, unless she exactly met the quota the slop-shop had set for her. Given that it had taken half a day to move, she would have to get straight to work.

She walked over to the sewing desk and set her bundle of fabrics, needle and thread upon it. For an instant, her heart quailed at the thought of sitting here hour upon hour, day upon day, making these mind-numbing clothes at a greater speed than ever, knowing with every waking moment that their survival was in her hands – now more than ever.

She had no choice. She threaded her needle, sorted out her fabrics, and got to work.

THE RAGGED SEAMSTRESS

TAYLOR WAS BEGINNING to wonder why he bothered with walking all the way to the livery anymore. His limbs ached; it had been another long, hard week – as they all were, truth be told – and he knew he could be lying stretched out in the hayloft right now, enjoying a rare afternoon nap, catching up on all the missing hours of sleep.

Instead, he was here, standing in front of the livery yard's gate, plucking up the courage to walk through that yard yet again and ask Mr. Goswick the same question he had been asking for the past six weeks. All he wanted was to learn; why the old man had to be so stingy with his knowledge was beyond Taylor's comprehension. London had taught him that this was simply the way of most men. They would give nothing away, not even a kind word, not even a spare glance or a smile.

But this was the only avenue he could think of that might lead him to May, and so he would have to keep chipping away at its dead end until it broke. Or perhaps it was time to give up on it all. He hesitated, glancing back in the direction of home, and thought of the pretty maid with her dark hair and dimpled smile. Was it worth it to throw away his whole life in pursuit of a girl who might not even remember him? Could he settle for less?

Perhaps he could.

He thrust his hands into his pockets against the chill breeze, and they brushed up against a small, soft object. Gently, he pried it out of his pocket. It was the little stuffed fox that May had made for him all those years ago.

Smiling to himself, Taylor fingered one of its worn ears. The fox was almost unrecognizable now. Years of love had faded its original colours; some of its seams had split, revealing the jumble of rags within. But he still knew it, no matter its sad appearance. It was a symbol of the first real kindness he had ever been shown in his life at that point.

He had to persevere. It was impossible to give up hope on a thing so precious.

Squaring his shoulders, Taylor strode into the yard. It was a little less busy today than the past few times; winter was setting in, and there were fewer pleasure riders about. Still, the hunting season would begin soon, and he guessed that the tall bay horse standing tied to a ring in the wall was a hunter from its sleek lines and lean body. A man was strapping it with strong movements – brushing its neck and shoulders firmly and briskly with a hard brush. The big muscles jumped under the horse's shining coat, loosening and strengthening from the effort.

Taylor watched admiringly for a few minutes. He had seen Mr. Hayes strap his master's hunter before, but this man had a wonderful technique. Glancing around, he saw that Mr. Goswick was occupied in his office. Coming up to the man, he said, "Good afternoon, sir."

The man glanced over his shoulder, not ceasing in his work. "Afternoon," he grunted.

Taylor swallowed but found some mettle in himself and spoke again. "How do you get his muscles to move in such a rhythm?"

The man glanced over at him. "Don't you know how to strap, lad? No wonder Mr. Goswick won't let you help him."

"I don't know very much, sir, but that's why I want to help," said Taylor eagerly. "I want to learn, and I know you and Mr. Goswick could teach me very much."

The man grunted, continuing with his strapping, and Taylor waited in silence for a few more moments. Finally, the man turned to him, holding out the hard brush.

"Show me what you can do," he said.

Eagerly, Taylor took the brush and approached the hunter, which gave him a disinterested look out of one eye. He touched its neck reassuringly and began to brush in smooth, hard strokes. The muscles twitched and jumped under his touch, but somehow, he just couldn't get the same result that the other man did.

"It's in your timing, lad," said the man. "Try to feel a rhythm."

Gritting his teeth, Taylor tried counting in his head, bringing the brush down like a metronome, and suddenly the horse's body began to play along. He laughed. "It's working."

"Well, look at that," said the man, and there was a note of begrudging respect in his tone.

"What is the meaning of this?" thundered Mr. Goswick's voice.

Immediately, Taylor stepped back, dropping the brush as though it had burned him. He whipped around. Mr. Goswick was standing mere inches away, arms folded, glaring at Taylor down a hooked nose.

"I'm s-sorry, sir," Taylor stammered. "I just saw this gentleman strapping, and I know I can't do it this well, and – "

"The lad took to it quick, sir," said the man.

"No one asked for your opinion, Percy," snapped Mr. Goswick.

Percy shrugged. "Well, I'll give it anyway," he said comfortably. "The boy just wants to learn. What harm could there be in letting him? He ain't asking for money, sir. Just a chance."

Mr. Goswick gave Taylor a long, contemplative stare, then turned to Percy. "I don't have time to educate some young fool for free."

"Well, I do," said Percy. "He can follow me around, and if all he does is carry water buckets, then it's one less thing I have to do, ain't it, sir?"

Mr. Goswick gave them both a long glare. Taylor realized his hands were trembling.

"Very well." He sighed. "But I'm warning you, boy, if you put one foot out of line, or cause me one ounce of trouble, or if I hear one peep of difficulty from you – that's the end of it. Do you understand?"

"Yes, sir. Thank you, sir. I won't let you down, sir," Taylor gushed.

Shaking his head, Mr. Goswick strode back to his office, and Percy picked up the brush and handed it back to Taylor.

"Go on then, lad," he said. "Finish the strapping."

Taylor turned and set back to his work with vigour. He thought of the little fox lying in his pocket and wondered if kindness was like luck; perhaps it followed charms around.

PART V

CHAPTER 16

Two Years Later

TAYLOR LEANED over the stable door, peering into the darkening interior. Sunset was coming more and more quickly these days, but there was still enough light for him to see the sleek hackney mare nibbling at her manger. She turned to look at him as he peered inside, and he felt a deep sense of satisfaction growing in his heart. Everything in that stable was exactly as it should be: the mare was wearing her striped blanket, standing deep on a bed of golden straw, her manger filled with hay, her bucket with water, her eyes bright and calm as she studied him.

"Good night, beauty," he told her, then stepped back for a last glance around the yard. It was cleanly swept, every head collar hung up, every rug folded. Ready for the day to begin tomorrow.

A swell of contentment grew in Taylor's chest. As soon as he returned home, he would do this all over again – feed and water the horses, set their boxes fair, sweep out the aisle, and go to bed knowing all was as it should be. Even though every bone in his body ached at the end of the day, it was a good day.

Taylor strode over to Mr. Goswick's office, whistling, his hands tucked into his pockets. He knocked gently on the window. Mr. Goswick looked up, beckoning irritably for him to come in. Taylor put his head around the door.

"All's well here, sir," he said. "That new mare ate up her supper, too."

"She did?" Mr. Goswick looked at him in surprise. "Why, Percy could hardly get her to eat a bite yesterday."

"I put a little treacle over it, sir. She was quite happy."

"Good to know." Mr. Goswick nodded. "Now go on home."

"Yes, sir. Thank you, sir."

"Don't thank me, just keep learning," snapped Mr. Goswick. "And shut the door properly on the way out. You're letting in an awful draught."

Taylor did as he was told and went his way quickly, suddenly aware that the sun was sinking dangerously fast toward the horizon and that it was only a matter of minutes before he was supposed to be back at the manor, putting their horses to bed. He jogged the last half-mile, hurrying breathlessly into the yard as dusk fell over the serene stable and outbuildings.

The stable lantern was glowing, and that brought Taylor up short as he walked toward its doors. Lighting the lantern was his task. A knot of discomfort gathered in his belly, and he approached the doors slowly, pulling them open.

"There you are, boy," growled Mr. Hayes. "About time, too."

Taylor's heart stuttered in his chest. Mr. Hayes was standing in the middle of the aisle, arms folded, a twisted look of anger and triumph on his face. Beside him was Master Harold – the master of the entire estate. He looked furious to be found down here in the stable, particularly at this hour on a Sunday.

"It's just as I told you, sir," said Mr. Hayes triumphantly. "The boy disappears at noon and only returns at the stroke of five, every Sunday afternoon for the past two years."

Taylor knotted his fingers together, squeezing them nervously. Master Harold looked none too pleased.

"What is the meaning of this, boy?" he demanded.

"Sir, I apologize," said Taylor, terrified. "I – I believed that twelve to five on a Sunday was still my afternoon off, but if it's changed – "

"That is your afternoon off. At least, it's meant to be," snapped Master Harold. "Yet Mr. Hayes here tells me that you have spent every moment of those five hours working at some common livery yard in the village."

Taylor stared at him, confused. "Sir, I'm not working for money, I'm just there to learn," he said nervously. "I've brought a lot of good knowledge back here to apply to your horses, sir."

"Oh, you have, have you?" roared Master Harold, spooking the horses so that they kicked and snorted in their stables. "So the education Mr. Hayes has been giving you hasn't been enough for you, has it?"

"No, sir, that's not what I meant," said Taylor.

"It's exactly what he means," Mr. Hayes whined. "He would rather learn from that dratted Quincy Goswick than from the horse master of one of the most prestigious families in the county."

"Oh, no, sir, that's not why I'm there." gasped Taylor.

"Well then, why are you there, boy?" snapped Master Harold. "I have no patience for your lies. You just said you were going to that run-down place to learn, and now you say you aren't."

"Sir, I've learned so much from Mr. Hayes," Taylor spluttered. "I just wanted to learn more about the livery business."

"Oh?" Master Harold's eyes glittered dangerously. "And why would that be, when you're working for a manor house? For any other stable lad that would be quite enough, boy, especially with the chance to replace Mr. Hayes one day when he grows old."

Mr. Hayes shot the master a quick, venomous glance at those words.

"Well, sir, I... I wanted to run my own livery someday," said Taylor helplessly.

"Oh, is that so?" Master Harold's voice dropped an octave with anger. "I suppose that my manor – my family's house – isn't good enough for you, is it?"

"No, sir..." Taylor began.

Master Harold silenced him with a swift, cutting motion of his hand. "I shall have no more of this, boy," he barked. "I have no patience for disloyalty. You are dismissed."

Taylor stared at him, stunned, unable to comprehend what he had just heard. "D-dismissed, sir?"

"I won't repeat myself. Make yourself scarce, or Mr. Hayes will see to it that you do," snapped Master Harold, storming out of the stable.

Taylor trembled to his bones. Dismissed. How was he meant to survive now? Where would he find food, shelter, the little money he had been tucking away each week for the sake of buying that horse of which he had dreamed for years?

How would he ever see May again?

He turned to Mr. Hayes for help, but he saw jealousy and rage in the eyes of the old stable master". "I'll give you time to fetch your things from the loft, boy, but only because I've no interest in clearing up your rubbish," he barked. "Take it and leave."

"Please, sir," Taylor stammered. "I've done nothing wrong."

"You've been disloyal," snapped Mr. Hayes. "Now go."

Taylor knew that no quarter would be given him now. He stumbled up the steps to the loft, gathering up his few possessions: another coat, a pair of socks, and a tiny pouch of money. It was with gratitude that he saw the money was still there.

When he stepped out of the stable for the last time, he realized with a shock that he'd had no time to say goodbye to the horses that had been his charges for the past four years. He turned to do so, but Mr. Hayes slammed the stable door shut, and he only had time to see Badger's old face looking at him before it was closed away from him forever.

Stunned, he turned and stared at what little he could see of the road ahead of him. It was completely dark now, and there was not a star in the sky to guide him. Reaching into his pocket, he fondled the shape of the tiny fox.

If ever he needed some kindness, it was now.

Mama was pale again this morning. She sat huddled on the sleeping pallet, a thin blanket draped around her shoulders, her face a terrible, ashen pallor in the faint light of the candle stub and the red glow from the fire. May knew she needed to get to work, or she would never make the quota she had been set, yet she had to care for her mother first.

She poured some tea into their one tin mug. There used to be two mugs, but when Mama had first fallen ill, May had taken everything they could spare to the pawnshop and sold it. One mug would have to do. The doctor had said, then, that he was uncertain what was wrong with her. He had given them medicine, but all it had done was to make her sleep. Still, perhaps that helped. She had seemed to have more colour in her cheeks for a week or two after that.

Now, that colour was gone, and there was a redness around her eyes that May was seeing more and more often lately. She crouched down in front of Mama, holding out the tea. "Here," she murmured. "Drink this. Perhaps you'll feel better."

Mama's eyes focused slowly on the tea, and she took it shakily. "Thank you, darling," she said. "Don't worry about me. Best you get to work."

"But you need to drink some tea, Mama," said May.

Mama nodded, taking a trembling sip. "I'm all right," she said. "I'll be all right."

"Perhaps you should try to sleep a little," said May.

She had never known Mama to sleep during the day – not before she had been taken ill. But now, Mama just nodded meekly, and May retired to her sewing desk.

She pulled out a sheaf of dark brown fabric and started cutting almost without needing to measure. She had made this same skirt so many times measuring was unnecessary. Everything within her cried out at the boredom of this movement, but she didn't hum; somehow, in the past two years, she had forgotten all of the hymns she had learned from that other tenement that had at least had a small window.

She longed for that tenement. She remembered leaning against the window and peering out at the street below, watching people go by; or just having short conversations through the curtain with their neighbours. Her heart ached for that breath of human company. The doctor and the pawnbroker had been the first people she had seen in months, the first time she had walked in sunlight for even longer. Candlelight and sewing had become her lot.

Now, for the past two weeks, Mama had been going out again, and May was enclosed once more in this cellar. She knew that Mama's intentions were to keep her safe, not to imprison her. Yet the walls seemed to be growing closer and closer around her with every day that passed.

She ran her scissors up the fabric in a smooth, practiced curve. If only she could make some of those little stuffed animals again. It had been years since the last time she had been able to make something herself; these days, every scrap of rag had to be sold to the rag-and-bone man if they were to afford both rent and candles, let alone food. She longed for the days when she had made tigers and lions, and cows and dogs, and bunnies and mice for the local children. It had been wonderful to be able to make something of her own, to bring out into the world something of the beauty she could find within herself. Better still had been seeing the expressions on the faces of the children when they were given her toys.

She would never forget Taylor's face the day she had given him that fox. He had been so young then, so frightened. Her heart ached within her for his company. Even making these intolerably dull clothes would have been all right if he could only be here, talking with her, brightening her world with his presence. It had taken six years for her to realize this, but she knew now that Taylor was dead. Mama had never been able to tell her outright, but she knew he had thrown himself from the docks and was gone.

The thought was crushing. She paused, staring down at the fabric, almost unable to summon the strength to go on cutting it. Snatching around for a spark of hope, she grasped the only one she could find.

"Have you had any luck finding another tenant to share the cellar with us, Mama?" she asked.

There was no response. May looked back. Mama was curled up on the pallet, sound asleep again.

She sighed deeply. She had been so hopeful when Mama had said that she wanted to find another tenant to join them, splitting the costs. It would help them eat every day, May thought, but best of all, it might give her some company during these long cold hours in this dark and lonely cellar.

It was a faint hope, but it was all that she had.

CHAPTER 17

THERE WAS ONLY one place Taylor could think of going, and even though he had walked this same path so many times over the past two years, it was still difficult to find the livery yard in the perfect blackness of the night. The two miles seemed to be an impassable distance, one that only stretched further and further ahead of him as he stumbled along the lane, bumping into the hedge from time to time, his arms held out in front of him, groping around trees and ditches as best he could.

With every stride, Taylor was painfully aware that this could be his lot in life from now on. He may have to sleep out here, perhaps beneath a hedge, perhaps with nothing but a hollow in the ground for shelter. He may spend night after night in this blackness, waiting for the sun to rise. There was no shelter here, not even a doorway or an alley as there had been in London. The thought of winter struck fear deep into his soul.

It seemed to take a terrifying eternity before he felt the familiar wooden fence on his right hand, and then, wonderfully, he was pulling back the latch and stumbling onto the beloved cobblestones of the livery yard. He shut the gate behind him, seeing a glimmer of light in the office. Mr. Goswick was still there; he lived in a small home behind the yard, Taylor knew, near the grooms' quarters. It was a relief that the office light was on. Taylor had begun to feel as though he was completely blind.

Almost tearful with relief, he staggered up to the door and thumped on it.

"Who's there?" Mr. Goswick snapped, his voice fearful.

"Oh, please, sir," Taylor gasped out. "It's me."

The door swung open, and Mr. Goswick stood moodily in the doorway, his eyes sweeping over Taylor's dishevelled appearance in one glance. He was gripping a walking stick in one hand as though it were a weapon.

"Don't you have other stables to see to, boy?" he barked.

"I've been dismissed, Mr. Goswick," Taylor panted. "Mr. Hayes found out I was helping you, and – "

"Patrick Hayes is a jealous old fool," snapped Mr. Goswick, "whom I dismissed from my yard many years ago for being an all-around idiot. It's no wonder he was angry when he found out you were working here."

"I didn't mean to cause any trouble, sir," Taylor cried. "But now – I – I'm on my own. I have nowhere to go. Oh, please, sir, please, don't you have a position for me?"

Mr. Goswick snorted and put a hand on the door as though to slam it shut. "I knew it would come to this. This is exactly why I didn't want you here in the first place, boy. I knew you would ultimately come begging for a position that I don't have for you."

"Please, sir, I'll do three times the work of any other lad," said Taylor desperately. "You know I know everything about this stable, I can handle customers, I can groom and exercise horses, I can do anything you please, sir. Please, give me a chance."

"Don't beg, boy," snapped Mr. Goswick. "It's unbecoming and fruitless. You know yourself that we have enough stable lads for all these horses."

"But there are three empty stables, sir," said Taylor desperately. "If you had three more horses, you could make more money. And I could be their stable lad. Weren't you just saying the other day how useful it would be to have a couple of big strong farm horses about? So often farmers have a lame or sick one and need to hire something for the day, and we never have anything suitable."

He was babbling and desperate now, but Mr. Goswick's eyes grew contemplative at his words. Stroking his chin, the old man looked him in the eye.

"All right, boy," he said finally. "I did say that, and I have been planning on it, and I'd rather not have to find some stupid child and have to train him from the start. But I was never planning on hiring a stable lad before I even have extra horses to pay his keep. You can come, but there will be no wages, do you understand? You'll sleep in the loft and you can eat with the others, but that's all."

Taylor stared at him for a second, feeling both hope and disappointment. At least he would not be sleeping beneath a hedge tonight. Still, he thought of his dream, of the horse he was going to buy and ride to London, of seeing May again.

May. His heart yearned for her.

"Of course," said Mr. Goswick, moving to close the door, "if you're not interested..."

"I am. I am," said Taylor quickly. "Thank you, sir. Thank you very much, sir."

"Go to bed and stop bothering me," snapped Mr. Goswick, slamming the door.

Taylor walked over to the loft, taking deep breaths. Sleeping warm was just the first step. He would find another way to see May again.

It was all he wanted, so he would have to.

※

"The new tenants are coming tonight," said Mama.

May looked up, startled, from the fresh new pile of fabric she was unfolding and sorting. Mama had just returned from another stint to the slop-shop and was busy brewing their first pot of tea in more than a day. There was some bread, too, and May's mouth watered for it — there had been no food last night — but she was still more excited to hear Mama's words.

"Oh, Mama, that's wonderful news." she said. "Where did you find them?"

"I saw them on the street. The mother was paging through a paper, trying to find a tenement, but one could tell she could barely read." Mama shrugged. "They're happy to share the rent."

"I'm so glad, Mama," said May eagerly. "What are they like?"

"They are like people who can save us half-a-crown each week, darling," said Mama shortly. She coughed and closed her eyes as though it was painful. May had thought that it was simple weakness that had made her take an extra hour for the journey to the slop-shop and back today; now, she hoped perhaps it was just because Mama had stayed to talk to these new tenants. Still, Mama's face was very pale, and her breaths were quick and short as she poured the tea.

"That's good," said May cautiously, trying a different tactic. "What do they do for work?"

"Mr. Glover works at a brickfield. Mrs. Glover and her daughter are match workers, and their eldest son is away at sea. They've just been turned out of their old tenement." Mama shakily held out the mug of tea. "So, they're quite desperate. I'm certain they will join us in the cellar."

"Oh, the poor things." said May, taking the mug. "How awful for them."

"Well, it's good for us," said Mama. Her face softened a little as she watched May take a sip of the tea. "Perhaps we won't have to sell the rags anymore, darling. You could make some of your own things again."

"I hope the daughter is nice," said May. "It would be so lovely to have someone to talk to again." She held out the mug to Mama. "Although you're always my favorite, Mama."

"That's sweet of you to say, darling." Mama laughed softly, but it turned into a painful cough. She took the mug and staggered over to the pallet, then sank down upon it and sipped slowly, her shoulders trembling with the effort of every breath.

THE TENANTS CAME AT TEN O' clock that night, shuddering their way into the cellar with wide eyes and pale faces. May was still piecing together the last hem of a skirt when Mama let them in. She set it aside quickly, her heart thudding with excitement at the sight of them.

Hungrily, her eyes swept their faces, taking them in. Mr. Glover was a stooped figure, with grossly enlarged hands and huge, dark eyes that seemed to be filled with suffering, but he nodded respectfully to Mama when they came inside; Mrs. Glover was a little mouse of a creature, her greying hair hanging around her face in ropes. And then there was a girl, about May's own age, with her father's sad dark eyes and her mother's broad, unsmiling mouth.

"Oh, hello." May rushed over to them, reaching out to grasp Mrs. Glover's hands. "I'm so glad that you're here."

"This is my daughter, May," said Mama, her voice tired.

Mrs. Glover blinked down at her hands and then up at May, as though she failed to understand why she was being touched without any intention of harm. "Hello," she said faintly.

"Sir, you look so tired," said May. "Please sit." She pushed her upturned bucket nearer. "And I see you've brought a pallet – here – let me help you put it in place. Is this corner all right?"

She hurried to and fro, helping Mr. Glover to set down the pallet, putting the kettle over the fire, taking a small box from the daughter, and setting it beside the fire. When she glanced into it, she saw that it contained what had to be all of their worldly possessions: three tin bowls, three mugs, three spoons, a spare blanket, which had a large rip in it.

May lifted the blanket from the box, turning to young Miss Grover. She kept her voice low so that Mama wouldn't hear her. "Miss? What's your name?"

The girl turned to her. When her eyes lit upon the blanket in May's hands, her cheeks flushed scarlet, and she snatched it away. "That's ours."

"I know," said May. "I was hoping you would let me mend it for you."

"We don't have money." The girl clutched the blanket a little more tightly.

May laid her hand over the girl's. "I wasn't going to ask you for any. I would just like to mend it for you."

Their eyes met then, and May saw that despite the darkness of the girl's eyes, they seemed to hold stars within them. They shone a little brighter now, and the broad mouth turned beautiful with a shy but genuine smile.

"Why?" she asked.

"Because it's not right for you to be cold."

The girl studied her a moment longer, then held out the blanket. "Eunice," she said. "My name's Eunice."

"I'm May." She took the blanket and grinned, and Eunice grinned back, and from that moment on, they were friends.

CHAPTER 18

Taylor sank gratefully onto the pile of hay, letting out a sigh of relief as he did so. Perhaps there were finer mattresses in the world, but he had never lain upon a bed more comfortable than this. The hay was fresh and springy beneath him; a little dusty, to be sure, but with a wonderful, sweet sunlight smell. Where he lay, he could gaze out of the little loft window at the silvery stars that graced the night sky, and beneath him were the contented sounds of horses at rest – the champ of hay being chewed, deep snorts, the soft thud as a horse lay down quietly on the straw.

He closed his eyes. The little pouch of his savings was still beside him and had not grown one ha'penny in the two months he had been working for Mr. Goswick. But at least his belly was full of rice. One could do some thinking on a full belly.

Mr. Goswick gave each boy one day off each week; Taylor's was a Thursday. He had been going down into the village every week, trying to find a way to make a little extra money, but the village was tiny and tight-knit, and every job seemed to be spoken for. Even the village idiot swept the market square. Maybe he needed to cast his net further afield, even go around to the manor houses and see if they needed shoes to be shined. He could even ask the local farrier to show him a few things about trimming hooves, but then again, the man already had an apprentice.

He just had to find a way to make enough money to buy a horse. Even the dullest, most ordinary horse could be hired out by the hour and make something. Even the slowest horse could take him to London to find May.

Her face filled his mind, and he was slowly drifting into dreams of her when there was a flurry of sound from below him. Opening his eyes, Taylor realized he was hearing horses getting to their feet, banging around in their stables, whinnying in confusion. He sat up with a jolt of fear. Could it be fire? But the air was clear, and the loft was dark, and there was no sign of smoke.

Groping for his lantern, Taylor scrambled down the loft's ladder in the dark – lighting a lantern in a hayloft would be unthinkable folly – and lit the lantern once he was standing in the yard. "What's wrong, beauties?" he called out to his horses.

They were all looking out of their stables, and Spark let out a sharp snort, her little ears pointed toward the gate. A moment later the latch rattled. Taylor swung the lantern in that direction, and the beam of golden light revealed a young man in neat but ordinary clothes, who was running toward Taylor with a pale face and wide eyes.

"Please. A horse. A horse." he cried. "I need a horse at once."

"It's very late, sir," said Taylor. "I don't think – "

"You don't understand." The young man wrung his hands. "My wife is having a baby, and there's something wrong. We need the doctor, but he's all the way over in the next village. I must ride for her life. Please, I beg of you, a horse."

Taylor's veins burned with the young man's urgency. "Run and knock on the office door," he said, hanging up the lantern. "Ask Mr. Goswick, but in the meantime, I will be saddling our fastest horse; you could be out of the gate in two minutes, sir."

The young man was running for the office before Taylor could finish speaking. He rushed to the tack room, pulling out a saddle and bridle belonging to their swiftest hunter, Skylark. The horse seemed to know at once that something was amiss when Taylor came bursting into his stable. He shifted impatiently, pawing at the ground as Taylor tightened the girth. He was jogging and pulling as Taylor led him out onto the yard.

The young man was shoving money into Mr. Goswick's hand in the door of the office. Taylor felt a pang of annoyance; surely the old man could have allowed payment in arrears, just this once. But the young man was running toward Taylor now, his hand still in his purse.

"I've never seen a horse saddled so quickly," he said. "Thank you, boy." With that he shoved a cold hard coin into Taylor's hands.

Taylor took it without thinking, gripping the reins tightly. "I'll leg you up, sir," he said. "You can go across country on this one; he'll jump anything, anything."

He boosted the young man swiftly into the saddle, and at once Skylark was away, flying across the yard and through the open gate. His hoofbeats rang on the road, and he disappeared into the night.

"Best start cooking a bran mash for that horse when he gets back, boy," Mr. Goswick shouted from the office door. "He'll be tired."

"Yes, sir," said Taylor.

He headed to the feed room, and only when he'd turned on the gas light and stepped inside did he remember about the coin that the young man had given him. He opened his hand, and it lay there in his palm: a shining round shilling.

Taylor's breath caught in his chest. A whole shilling. He closed his fist over it again, gazing contemplatively out at the empty yard.

Sometimes the rich could be grateful if one went the extra mile, he realized. It seemed that it was that extra mile where the potential for saving some money lay.

***

MAMA WAS SHIVERING. May crouched down, grasping the blanket, and pulled it snugly over her shoulders where she lay on the pallet. It was so strange to look down at Mama like this; her face grey and hollow, her eyes closed. She hadn't noticed how terribly deep Mama's eye sockets had become, deep pits among the bony edges of her face. When she rested her hand on Mama's shoulder, it was jagged and sharp, emaciated against her palm.

"Oh, Mama," May whispered, hooking some of Mama's grey hair back from her face. Should she send for the doctor again? She felt Mama's forehead, trying to determine if she was feverish or just cold. Things were a little better now that the Glovers were sharing the rent, but not by much. The price of candles had risen. May didn't know which she should choose – food or medicine.

Tears hovered behind her eyes. She should never have let Mama go out to buy coal, food and candles all alone today, but she was working so hard to meet the slop-shop's ever-rising quota. She couldn't have taken even half an hour away from her work without consequences. If she had gone instead of Mama, though, her mother could have stayed safely down here in the nice warm cellar instead of stumbling around in the elements...

May blinked, rubbing at her exhausted eyes. They were so sore and strained from staring down at her sewing all day in the flickering candlelight, but she would have to get another hour or so out of them, to get ahead on her quota. That way, she could go out for candles tomorrow, if it was necessary.

"Please get better, Mama," May whispered, bending down to kiss her mother's forehead. "You just need to get better."

Mama stirred on the pallet, muttering.

"What was that?" May leaned closer. "Did you say something, Mama?"

Mama rolled over, tugging the blanket with her, and muttered again. This time, May heard it quite clearly: it was a name. It sounded like "Ludwig". She frowned. She'd never heard that name before. Mama must be dreaming.

"Shh." May stroked the blanket down over Mama's shoulder. "Just rest now."

She got up and returned to her sewing desk, and had just begun to slowly sew, her tired eyes struggling to pick out the stitches in the fading light, when the door opened, and the Glovers came in. They always returned terribly late; Eunice and Mrs. Glover's shift at the match factory only ended around eight or nine, and then they had to walk all the way home, too. It was about ten o' clock now, not an unusual time for them to get home, but that was where the ordinary ended. Instead of shuffling inside, subdued, starving and exhausted, the Glovers were chattering excitedly among each other.

"Hello," May said, hurrying across the room. "It's good to see you all – but please – Mama just fell asleep at last."

"Sorry, dear," whispered Mrs. Glover, who certainly looked different. Her eyes were shining. She reached out and squeezed May's hands. "We're all just so excited."

"It's so good to see you all smiling," said May, looking up at Mr. Glover, who was grinning beneath his bushy grey moustache. "What's the occasion?"

"May, it's so wonderful." Eunice hissed in excitement, pushing past her parents to grip May's hands. "Ralph is home."

For the past few weeks, Eunice had spoken of nothing except her brother. He was due to arrive home at the end of the month after spending almost a year at sea.

"Oh." May gasped. "That's wonderful."

"Yes." Eunice turned, reaching back into the doorway. "Here he is."

She gripped an unseen hand and pulled her brother into the warm light of the cellar, and May felt her heart do a strange little stutter in her chest. Ralph Glover was nothing like she had imagined. She had been picturing a male version of Eunice, but the boy standing in front of her was taller even than his father, and his black hair was long and wild over his shoulders. He smelled inexpressibly good – there was salt and tar and sea wind in his scent, but something else too, something wild and exotic. His eyes were the brightest blue, and they danced as they rested on May, his mouth stretching into a familiar broad smile.

"Hello," he said, his voice deep and rumbling. "You must be May. Eunice has told me so much about you since we met at the docks."

"I am," May stammered, feeling the blood creep up her cheeks. "I – hello. Yes. I'm May."

Eunice giggled, clinging to her brother's arm. "You should hear the stories Ralph has to tell," she gasped. "This is the third time he's been to sea, and he's always got the most amazing things to tell us. Oh, Ralph, did you see monkeys again this time?"

"I did," said Ralph. "Come on – let's eat, and I'll tell you everything." He held up a paper bag, spotted with grease, that smelled incredible. "Would you like to join us, May?"

May stepped back. The bag smelled so good, but she had already eaten, and she and Eunice had long since made a pact not to impose on one another when it came to food; they were both penniless. "Oh, no thank you, Ralph. I'm – "

"May, it's all right." Eunice gripped her hand. "Ralph made much more money on the ship than he thought."

May looked up at Mr. Glover, who nodded benevolently.

"Let's eat," said Ralph. "I'm starving."

They all sat down by the fire and helped themselves to fat handfuls of hot, sticky chips, and they were the most delicious thing May had ever eaten. Ralph was smiling at her, and offering her more, and she liked it.

But all the time, she couldn't quite stop thinking about Taylor.

***

MAMA PUSHED THE BLANKET DOWN, struggling to sit up. "Let me go, May," she croaked feebly. "You have work to do."

"I do, but I'll do it tonight, Mama," said May stubbornly. "I'm not letting you go out in the rain."

Exhausted by the simple action of sitting up, Mama glared at May, her chest heaving with effort. She coughed a few times, and May laid a hand on her shoulder. Rain droned on the roof, sounding distant and muffled.

"It's pouring out there, and cold," said May softly. "You can't go out. The damp and cold will be so bad for you, and you're not well."

"I'm all right," Mama croaked.

"The doctor said you should be kept warm and dry," said May.

She cast a grateful glance over to the corner of the cellar, where Eunice and Ralph were busy putting on their coats. Mr. and Mrs. Glover were at work, but Ralph had insisted on taking Eunice away from the factory and had given her a little money. In turn, Eunice had asked the doctor to see Mama, and paid him too.

If only the doctor had been able to give them some kind of cure. Instead, he'd given Mama more of the medicine that made her sleepy and told May she should be kept indoors.

"You can't go out in this," Mama protested. "You'll be taken ill, too."

"I won't. Ralph and Eunice said they're coming too, and Ralph has an umbrella," said May, excited. She'd never walked under an umbrella before; they had never been able to afford one. "It'll all be fine, Mama, but please stay here, take your medicine, and rest."

Mama hung her head. "I'm sorry, darling."

"Don't be sorry." May kissed her forehead. "It's not your fault. I'll bring you back something to eat, and you'll feel much better soon."

She prayed this was the case as she followed Ralph and Eunice out of the cellar and onto the street. The rain came down in a quiet gray curtain; she braced herself for the burst of cold over her head, but as she stepped forward, Ralph held out his umbrella, and she heard the patter of rain on it instead.

"Oh." She gasped, looking up at him. "This is wonderful."

Ralph laughed, and he was very close to her, his arm almost around her as he held the umbrella over the three of them. His smell was heady; she wondered why it still lingered upon him when he had been away from the ship for days.

"Let's go find something to eat," he said.

They walked to the market square, but not the sad, shabby one where May normally bought crusts of bread, watery soup, mouldy vegetables and soft potatoes for her and Mama. Instead, this market square had real shops around it, with glass windows and brick walls instead of tattered roofs made from sticks and rags.

The dreadful hunger that had been gripping May for years had lifted to such an extent that she was able to look all around instead of keeping her gaze locked on the fresh bread in the baker's window. There was a millinery on the far corner, and she caught a tantalizing glimpse of light and colour.

"Wait here," said Ralph, handing the umbrella handle to Eunice. "I'll get us some bread."

"Please, Ralph," said May, digging in her pocket, "would you get some bread for Mama, too?" She held out a thrupenny bit.

"Of course." Ralph took it. "I'll be right back."

He slipped into the shop, and Eunice giggled.

"What are you laughing at?" asked May.

"You," said Eunice. "You're making sheep's eyes at him."

"Sheep's eyes. What nonsense," said May. "I'm just hungry."

"I'll say," said Eunice, giggling again.

"Eunice." May joined in with the giggling, then looked longingly at the millinery again. "Can we go over to the millinery, and look at the dresses, while Ralph is in there?"

"Of course," said Eunice. "Come on."

Arm-in-arm under the umbrella, the two girls walked over to the shop. May didn't think it would be this close to the slums if it was fancy, but to her, it still seemed a wonderland of colour and beauty. She could barely breathe as she gazed through the glass.

There were dresses in there with all kinds of beautiful fabrics – taffeta, silk, chiffon, lace, satin, muslin – in all sorts of brilliant colours: greens and golds and blues and one vividly scarlet. May would have made the scarlet one a slightly softer tone and added ribbons along the bodice. The idea formed in her mind, bright as a picture, and she imagined being the lucky milliner who was at that moment taking the measurements of a pretty young girl in front of a big mirror. The girl had lovely dark green eyes. What a perfect dress May could make for her, in that same shade, with flowing lines that would complement her curves.

"It's so beautiful," she breathed.

"I know," said Eunice. "I wish I could have a dress like that, someday."

"I wish I could make a dress like that," said May.

"You *are* funny, May." Eunice tugged at her arm. "Come on. Let's go back to get my brother."

They turned, and that was when May saw him. Taylor. He was standing across the square with his back to her, looking at a display of hats in a window. Everything within May trembled. It had been so long, but surely, she would recognize him. Surely that tall, willowy figure belonged to a wiry boy, now grown up into a young man. Surely that neatly-cropped head of hair could belong to him…

She stumbled forward into the rain.

"May," Eunice gasped. "Where are you going?"

May barely heard her. The only thought in her mind was Taylor, to grasp his hand again, to look up into those soft brown eyes again. To be near her dearest friend again. She heard herself cry his name as she reached him, extending a hand, touching the back of his arm.

He turned, and May's heart played a wild crescendo in anticipation of seeing her old friend at last. But the young man who looked down at her was not Taylor at all. He had an imperious hook nose, and pale grey eyes that narrowed with irritation when they rested upon her.

"Don't touch me, wench," he spat, pulling back his arm.

"May!" Eunice had reached her. She grabbed her arm.

"I... I'm sorry, sir," May breathed. "I thought..."

"Filthy wretch. You must be mad," snapped the young man. "You should be in a lunatic asylum, not out on the streets."

"Leave her be." The deep, commanding voice belonged to Ralph. He strode up to them, putting a protective hand on May's shoulder. "She is no more insane than you are, and you're a hot-headed fool for suggesting it."

The young man looked Ralph up and down, his eyes dwelling on the broad shoulders and strong arms, and he thought better of saying anything. Instead, he gave May a last sidelong glance and strode away.

"Are you all right, May?" asked Eunice.

"I thought..." May's eyes were filling with tears. "I thought it was Taylor. I thought I'd found him."

"Oh, darling," said Eunice, wrapping her arms around her.

May sobbed wholeheartedly, her soul wrenched with loss. But even as she wept, she was acutely aware of Ralph's hand on her shoulder, and the strong presence of him beside her, and the smell of the sea.

CHAPTER 19

Mr. Goswick ran a finger down the list written on the large blackboard in front of his office. "Hmm, Mr. Wulfric is going to take Skylark out on the hunt tomorrow," he said thoughtfully. "It's a pity, because Lord Tennyson has asked to hire a good hunter for a guest, and I would have liked to impress him."

"How about Dart, sir?" asked Taylor. "She's a little gentler than Skylark and would suit any rider. After all, we don't know how well the guest rides. Dart is forgiving of any kind of hand."

Mr. Goswick grunted. "I didn't ask for your opinion, boy," he muttered, but scrawled Dart's name on the blackboard, nonetheless. Each stable lad had a list of horses that needed to be prepared for clients every day, and it gave Taylor a little thrill of satisfaction to see his name written out at the top of the board; he couldn't read much, truth be told, but he had learned to recognize the shape of his name and the names of most of the horses.

"Oh, yes," Mr. Goswick added as an afterthought. "And I want you to prepare Raven for me tomorrow morning. I'm riding down to London for the livestock sale. We need to fill those stables if you're going to earn your keep – and then some." He grunted with resentment as he wrote.

"To London, sir?" Taylor asked.

"Yes, there's a good sale on Saturday. I'll leave on Friday and come back on Saturday afternoon. I expect you to pack some rope halters into Raven's saddlebags, too, so that I can lead two new horses back."

Taylor hardly heard anything his master had said. His mind was filled instantly with thoughts of what London meant, which to him was one thing: May. If he could persuade Mr. Goswick to take him along, perhaps there would be time to slip away on Friday evening, to find her tenement...

"Sir, don't you think I should come along, too?" he said cautiously. "It will be a lot to manage, bringing two horses back while riding Raven."

"That's exactly why I chose her, boy," spat Mr. Goswick impatiently. "Raven will behave, and I won't buy anything that can't be easily handled."

"Still, sir, wouldn't it be safer..." Taylor attempted.

Mr. Goswick turned and scorched him with a furious glance. "I know you're not really interested in helping, so you may as well stop pretending," he spat. "You're just a simple boy wanting to see the big city, and you certainly will not do so at my expense. Stay here, keep your nose clean, and pray that the farmers will hire these animals as you suggested – or you'll find yourself out of a job."

The prospect sent a jolt of fear burning down into Taylor's stomach. He ducked his head, trying to swallow the bitter disappointment. "Yes, sir. I'm sorry, sir."

"Don't be sorry, just go back to work," barked Mr. Goswick.

Taylor scurried off, his heart aching. Never had May felt so close and yet at the same time so far.

※

MAY TUCKED the blanket more securely around Mama's shoulders. "Try to sleep, Mama," she said softly. "You need your rest."

Mama blinked up at her with reddened eyes, a withered claw tugging at the blankets. It was difficult to see her, now, as the invincible titan that May had known her to be when she was still a little child. She seemed a husk of the woman she had been then; her eyes were rheumy and dull, but when she wrapped May's hand in hers, the fervency of her tender love still shone in the gentle grip.

"Your work, darling," Mama croaked. "Don't stop."

"Of course not, Mama. But I've finished all I need for today. The lantern that Ralph bought us has made everything much quicker and easier."

Mama blinked up at her. "Ralph is a good man," she murmured. "And he likes you."

May felt her cheeks burning. She glanced over her shoulder toward the fireplace, where Ralph and Eunice were facing one another over a game of noughts-and-crosses scratched out with charcoal on the floor.

"Yes," she said quietly. "He is."

"The kind of man who could save you from this life," Mama added in a whisper.

May's thoughts strayed to Taylor again, the way they so easily did. But there they found only crushing sorrow and aching disappointment. She remembered the way she had felt when she had run up to that young man on the street, and he had turned to look down at her, and his eyes had been blue instead of brown. A qualm of agony shuddered through her heart.

Taylor was gone, and she would have to find a way to live with that knowledge. Perhaps Ralph could be that way.

"Yes," she said again. "I think he might be."

A faint smile crossed Mama's face, and it soothed her grief just to see that rare expression in her mother's eyes. She bent down to kiss her cheek, tucked up the blanket tightly, and went to join Eunice and Ralph by the fire.

Eunice was just drawing the last of three noughts. "Aha," she said. "I have you now."

"How do you keep doing that?" laughed Ralph, equal parts exasperated and amused. "Just as I think I'm about to win, you make a sneaky move like that one, you deceiving little vixen."

"Oh, there's only one person who can beat me at noughts-and-crosses," said Eunice. She looked up at May. "Care to play?"

"Yes, please," said May. "I'll show you how it's done, Ralph."

"Be my guest." Ralph grinned up at her, and his beautiful eyes were sparkling, filled with a hope that could lead her to the future. As he stood up to allow her to take his place, he trailed his fingertips lightly along her back, and a wonderful shudder crept down her spine.

She sank down opposite Eunice, rubbed out the last game's noughts and crosses, and they began to play. As usual, May played crosses, and she beat Eunice in four moves. Ralph laughed in delight as Eunice threw down her charcoal in mock despair.

"I can hardly believe it," he said.

"It's all the creative thinking," said Eunice. "She can imagine anything. Now, who wants some tea?"

"Oh, yes please," said May. Ralph agreed, and Eunice got up, lifting the kettle from the stove and going over to the makeshift table to pour the tea.

As soon as Eunice was out of earshot, Ralph came to sit down beside May, and his eyes held something both excited and contemplative. He reached toward her, a little hesitantly, and took her hand. May felt no urge to pull away. Ralph gave a little shudder of delight, grasping her hand in both of his own with a gentle touch, and looked into her eyes.

"May, there's something I have to tell you," he said.

May's heart fluttered within her. "What is it?"

"I spoke with the captain of the ship I usually work on yesterday. I started as a cabin boy, but as the time has passed, I have become more and more of a sailor. Now, the old quartermaster has retired, and I am to take his place." Ralph took a deep breath. "It means that there will be more money – much more money. I have been saving all my life, and this means that I can use my savings to rent a good house for my family, and Mama and Papa can be made more presentable and find better work. Eunice, too. There will be no more factories and no more dreadful tenements like this one."

May stared at him. Part of her had expected a declaration of the love she saw in his eyes each time he watched her walk across the room, but this... She barely knew how to feel about what he had just told her. Of course, there was a surge of joy in her heart for all of the Glovers, especially sweet Eunice, to escape this abysmal poverty.

But she knew this meant leaving her behind. The thought of being left in this cellar, alone with her sick mother, penniless once more, was more than she could bear.

"Ralph, that's wonderful," she said, but her voice cracked, and she had to turn her face away.

"That's not all, my sweet May." Ralph reached out and touched her chin softly with his fingertips, turning her head so that he could look into her eyes. "I... I have never felt about anyone the way I feel about you," he said quietly. "Your kindness, your grace, your creativity – you are... more than I can describe." He paused. "I want you to come with my family. I... I want you to be my wife, if you'll have me."

May's heart stuttered within her. She had misunderstood. Ralph was not leaving her behind in this poverty – he was saving her from it.

"Oh, Ralph." she gasped, tears of joy stinging her eyes. "Oh, I – "

"Wait. Before you are overjoyed... before you say anything." Ralph held up a hand. "It is only fair for me to tell you the full truth. I... I would be stretching my resources quite far to rent a home big enough for all of us... let alone feed everyone until better work can be found." He bit his lip, his eyes sliding to the side. "May, I would love to marry you, but I cannot provide for your mama."

May's heart turned suddenly to ice within her chest. She pulled her hand back, clutching it to her heart as though Ralph had burned it.

"I'm sorry," he said, a plea in his voice. "I cannot. I would if I could. I have to put my own parents first, and I know there is a risk that neither they nor Eunice will ever find work, nor you... and if that is the case, I cannot support them all. I have to be responsible. May, please, don't hate me."

"I could never hate you," said May softly. She thought of Mama, and the Jacksons, and realized that she understood for the very first time. She raised her eyes to Ralph's. "I want to come with you. With Eunice." She had to pause as her throat tightened with grief: they might have been sisters. "But I can't leave my mama."

"I didn't think you could... but my heart compelled me to ask." Ralph dropped his gaze, his cheeks reddening. "I'm sorry, May."

"I know you are," said May. "But I don't hate you. If things had been any different..."

The implication hung in the air between them, unspoken. Things were not different. And for May, it seemed, they never would be.

Taylor knew something was amiss the moment Mr. Goswick came across the yard, muffled in a thick coat and scarf, his hat pulled down low over his ears. The old man emitted a painful cough as he trailed toward Taylor where he stood holding Raven, the quiet black riding horse he'd saddled for Mr. Goswick's journey to London.

"Sir, are you all right?" Taylor asked.

"I'm fine, boy," snapped Mr. Goswick, but his voice came out as a hoarse rasp.

"You're very pale."

"Codswallop," snapped Mr. Goswick. "Give me that mare."

Raven sniffed him nervously, as though she was as unconvinced as Taylor. With a grunt of effort, Mr. Goswick hoisted his bag into the saddlebags and secured it.

"Perhaps Percy should go instead," said Taylor. "I'm sure he'd choose good horses, too."

"I told you, boy, there's nothing wrong with me," barked Mr. Goswick. He shoved a foot into the stirrup and hoisted himself up, but before he could swing a leg over the mare's rump, he emitted a low groan and sank back to the ground. For a moment, the old man swayed, and Taylor grabbed at his arm to keep him from falling.

"Don't touch me, boy." Mr. Goswick shook off his grip, but his voice lacked its usual intensity.

"Sir, you're not well," said Taylor, scared.

"Don't look so frightened. It's just a touch of cold." Mr. Goswick stepped back and stood panting for a moment, an unhealthy sweat upon his brow. "All the same... perhaps a ride to London would be unwise, after all."

"I think so, sir," said Taylor fervently.

"No one asked you." Mr. Goswick wiped his brow. "It's a pity. A friend in London tells me there are several horses on the sale that would be very suitable, and he thinks the prices will be good, too. This is not an opportunity to be missed."

"You could send Percy, sir," said Taylor.

"Percy," snorted Mr. Goswick. "How am I to keep a livery yard running without my stable master if I'm unwell? Can't you see I'm ill, boy?"

Taylor decided that it was best to remain silent when Mr. Goswick was in a mood such as this one. The old man watched him for a few seconds, puffing painfully, then placed his hands on his hips.

"Well, I suppose you'll just have to go, then," he said.

Taylor stared at him. "I beg your pardon, sir?"

"You heard me," said Mr. Goswick irritably. "You've as good an eye for a horse as anyone, and it's you who will be responsible for these horses, isn't it?"

Taylor was speechless for a moment, partly from surprise that Mr. Goswick would trust him with purchasing new horses, partly from sheer overwhelming joy that he was going to London after all.

"Well, don't just stand there." barked Mr. Goswick. "Get your things and go, or you'll be late."

"Thank you, sir. Thank you." Taylor gasped.

"Hurry up," snapped Mr. Goswick.

Taylor bolted for the hay loft, grabbing his few possessions. His hand closed around his little pouch of money. It turned out that some of the clients could be quite generous with tips if one was willing to bend over backward for them, but his savings still weren't much.

Yet perhaps they would be enough.

He ran back down to the yard, laughing with excitement. He was going to London. He was going to see May at last.

***

May hugged Eunice for a long time, weeping into her friend's hair. Eunice was clinging to her tightly, her voice broken.

"I'll come and see you, May," she sobbed out. "We'll find each other again, I know we will. I'm so sorry."

"Don't be sorry. Don't be sad," said May. She pulled back, her hands on Eunice's shoulders, and summoned a smile with all the courage she had left. "You're going to have a wonderful new life, Eunice, and you deserve every moment of it."

Eunice wiped at her eyes. "But I'll miss you so much."

"You won't. You'll be too busy enjoying all the good things in your life," said May. "Please, be happy for me. Don't miss me. Just live and be happy."

Eunice's eyes were shining with tears. "I'll try," she whispered.

"Eunice." Mrs. Glover put a hand on her daughter's arm and gave May a quick smile; she was shining with excitement. "The cab is here. It's time to go to our new home."

Eunice turned away, allowing her mother to lead her away to the waiting hansom-cab, and May knew that everything was going to change for the Glovers. She was sure that, like herself, Eunice had never even been in a carriage before. Her heart sang for her friend but was shattered for herself.

A light touch on her shoulder made her turn around. Ralph stood beside her, his eyes filled with mixed hope and grief.

"It's not too late to change your mind, you know," he said.

"I can't," May whispered. "I'm sorry."

"I love you for it," said Ralph. He took her hand, raised it to his lips, and gave it a kiss that was as lingering as it was gentle. "Perhaps things will be different when I return. If they are, I will come and find you."

"Perhaps," said May. "I hope so."

Ralph blinked, turning his face away, and May knew he was holding back his tears. He reached into his pocket and pulled out a scrap of paper and a small canvas purse. "Here," he said, shoving them into her hands.

The purse was heavy and clinked. "Ralph, no," said May.

"Please. Let me do this one thing for you." Ralph's voice was rough with tears. "Our new address is written on the paper. If it changes, I will write to you... your mama can read. Please. Come and find me, when you can."

"I will," said May.

Then he pulled away from her and was gone, disappearing into the cab. May stared after it as it drove off into the fog, but no one waved.

CHAPTER 20

It was so strange to see these streets from horseback.

Taylor rose and fell easily to Raven's rhythmic movement as the mare trotted along the street, her ears flicking this way and that at the chaotic surroundings. He had learned to ride bringing horses in for Master Harold from the far paddocks, and fallen his fair share of times, but now it came to him as naturally as breathing. Still, his muscles ached from the hours of riding from the village and cried out for a hot bath and a long rest – Mr. Goswick had given him enough money to book a place in an inn, which was something he had never done before. He'd suggested an inn close to the auction. It was exciting.

Far more exciting, however, was the prospect of seeing May again. He touched Raven with his heels, sending the mare forward into the gathering crowd. It had not taken him long to find his way back to his old neighbourhood, and he was nearly there now. The streets were growing narrower; Raven's iron-rimmed hooves had rung on stone just a few minutes ago, but now squelched in mud. There were no horses to be seen here. Only a few ragged donkeys, and many people afoot.

Taylor had the uncomfortable feeling that everyone was watching him. He kept a firm grip on the reins.

Ahead of him, the street opened up a little, and Taylor slowed Raven to a walk. They were stepping into a market square that was so familiar it almost felt as though no time had passed at all since he had last been here, even though it had been six years. The same tatty stalls lined the muddy square; the same bony stray dogs and cats scavenged among the rags and bones; the same awful smells rose from the crowded cluster of run-down sellers – bland gruel, rotten meat, mouldy vegetables, sour milk, and a quiet, pervasive stench of human waste.

It was the smell of poverty, and suddenly Taylor yearned for his clean hayloft and the country air.

But no amount of clean air could make up for how much he missed May. He looked up, beyond the market square, to the tenement building that had once been the only home where he had known love. Excitement surged through him, and he clicked his tongue to Raven and rode toward it.

The journey on horseback was far quicker than afoot, and Taylor only realized he'd gone past their old building when he recognized the workhouse up ahead. Puzzled, he turned Raven around, riding back through a crowd of sour-faced pedestrians. There was the neighbouring building – and there was the space where their old tenement building had been.

Taylor's heart froze within his chest.

The building was gone. Not even rubble remained; only an empty lot, with a few scraps of rubbish strewn across it, and sickly yellow grass growing up between the cracks in what had once been the foundation of his home.

Nausea rose bitterly in Taylor's stomach. He had never even contemplated the possibility that May might not be where he had left her. Dismounting from Raven, he hooked the mare's reins over one arm and stumbled over to the corner where their tenement had been.

Six years ago, he had stood in this same place, three stories up, and looked into May's soft blue eyes for the last time.

Dismay choked his throat. Taylor pressed the heels of his hands into his temples, trying to hold back tears. How would he ever find her now?

Raven nudged him, puzzled, and he lowered his hands, taking deep breaths. It was getting dark; he needed to reach the inn soon, or risk having the mare stolen and whisked off to some unthinkable fate in this heartless city. But there was one more place he could think to look for May.

He swung back up onto Raven's back and rode toward the workhouse, looking for the alley. It was almost too narrow to ride down, and he had to turn his toes forward to keep his boots from being scraped on the brick walls either side of him. His heart thudded as they rounded the turn.

May wasn't there. Only an empty dead end, and a brick wall lined with iron spikes.

Mama thrashed on the sleeping pallet, flinging her arms to the side. "No," she sobbed out, her back arching so that her ribs jutted painfully through her threadbare dress. "No, Ludwig, don't go."

"Hush, Mama, hush," May whispered in terror, squeezing water from the rag in her hand and gently using it to sponge Mama's sweaty brow. "Hush now."

"I need you," Mama sobbed out. "Ludwig, I need you."

"It's all right, Mama." May glanced desperately at the medicine bottle on her sewing desk. It was empty; beside it, the day's sewing lay strewn over the desk, ignored and undone. "Just try to sleep. Try to sleep."

Mama was asleep, but she seemed to find no rest in it. Her breath had a terrible rattle to it as she sucked in great, nervous gasps, her bony limbs thrashing as she turned over with a low, awful moan that ended in coughing.

"The Turners... the Turners," she muttered. "The Turners did this."

May was growing to fear that name. Mama had said it so many times in the past few days as she muttered in her feverish sleep, and May didn't know what any of it meant.

Now, Mama seemed to be quietening. She settled down to taking deep breaths, and May tugged the blanket up over her shoulders again. "That's it," she soothed. "Sleep, Mama, sleep." She touched Mama's brow, hoping the fever was breaking, but her skin was still scorching to the touch.

As she rested her hand on Mama's brow, the reddened eyelids fluttered. May held her breath, hoping to lull her back to sleep, but Mama was waking up. She looked up at May with rheumy eyes, coughed once, and reached up gently to rest bony fingertips on May's cheek. "You've been crying," she croaked. "Why?"

"Oh, no, Mama," said May, forcing a smile. "It's just the smoke from the fireplace."

In truth, May had done little other than cry in the week since Ralph and Eunice had left. Mama was so ill that she had barely noticed their leaving; May didn't know how to find other tenants, and knew she couldn't ask Mama to do it. And so, the little stash of money that Ralph had given her was dwindling by the day as she struggled to nurse Mama and to get her work done at the same time.

Mama was looking up at her with more brightness than usual. "Is it Ralph?" she whispered. "I can't believe he would just leave you, after the way you felt about him."

"No, no," said May. She hadn't been able to tell Mama about Ralph's proposal, because Mama would have made her take it, made her leave. May couldn't do that.

Mama closed her eyes. "It's not fair," she murmured.

"Mama, can I ask you something?" said May, brushing some of Mama's sweaty hair back from her face.

"Yes," Mama breathed.

May paused, biting her lip. "Who is Ludwig? And who are the Turners?"

Mama's eyes snapped open with disconcerting speed. She glared up at May, her hands trembling on the blankets. "Who told you about them?" she cried, in a rasping shriek.

"No one. No one, Mama." May shrank back. "You – you just said their names in your sleep, that's all."

Mama stared at her for a few moments longer, but exhaustion was leeching the fury from her gaze. Her eyes began to close.

"They're no one," she whispered. "No one at all."

Her breathing turned deep and slow, and May felt her forehead again. She was burning up. Looking down at her mother, at the skeletal hollows of her eyes, the deep scoops of emptiness beneath her collarbone, May knew Mama didn't have long unless she did something.

She scrambled to her feet and seized Ralph's purse, then hurried out into the street.

***

Taylor knew he should be satisfied. Mr. Goswick's friend had been right; the horses were going for excellent prices, and he had been able to buy a pair of excellent young draft horses at a fraction of the usual price, well within Mr. Goswick's budget. He knew that the old stable master would be pleased – might even give Taylor a little money for his efforts.

Yet no amount of money or approval could make up for the hollow burning in his heart.

Taylor sat disconsolately among the crowd gathered by the side of the auction ring as they bid on a shaggy little pony. The pony had one blue eye, and it reminded him of May, but then again everything he saw reminded him of May right now. Where could she have gone? How could he even begin to find her? He had kept his eyes peeled as he rode to the sale, looking for any street vendors with stuffed animals, looking through the window of every toy shop he passed. But there were none that looked like May's. Would she still be making stuffed animals? Would they look different, six years of skill later? Taylor didn't know, and it ate at his soul that he could not find her.

"This next lot is a real bargain, folks." the auctioneer was saying as the pony was led away. "A young colt, only three years old, ready to be broken in. You'll see plenty of potential here."

Judging from the disappointed mutters of the crowd as the colt was led into the ring, no one believed him, and at first glance Taylor felt more pity than excitement. The colt was a scrawny thing, with a giant head drooping on a long, thin neck wreathed in wild, tangled mane. His hip bones stuck out left and right; his back was long and weak, and his untrimmed hooves made his legs look pathetically thin.

"Five pounds," called the auctioneer. "Who'll give me five pounds?"

Taylor's hand tightened on his pouch. He only had a single pound and some change; it had seemed like all the money in the world at one point, but it wasn't horse-buying money.

"Four. Four pounds. Who'll give me four?"

The colt raised his giant head and looked quietly over the fence at Taylor. The movement raised his bushy forelock, and for the first time, Taylor saw his eyes. They were very large, fine and clear, with soft, limpid depths. Blinking at him, Taylor realized that the colt's nostrils were large and clean, too; his head had a chiselled look about it, like that of a thoroughbred racehorse. When the handler tugged at his halter and forced him to walk on, his stride looked awkward because of his big feet, but there was still a prowling energy to it that told Taylor he would be able to cover many a mile in comfort.

There *was* potential in this colt, after all. Taylor imagined him clean and well-fed with his mane pulled and his hooves neatly shod, and excitement ran through him.

"Two pounds. Come on, ladies and gentlemen. Who'll give me two pounds?"

There was some disgruntled muttering from the gathered buyers, and the auctioneer was beginning to look desperate.

"There's no reserve price, folks. Make your bid. Who'll give me one pound?"

Taylor jumped to his feet, a hand shooting into the air.

"One pound. One pound I'm bid. Who'll give me a guinea?"

There was total silence. The auctioneer shook his head and sighed, tapping the hammer.

"Sold to the young gentleman."

Taylor's heart thudded in his chest as he watched his colt being led away. He was here in London. He had bought his horse.

And yet still the most important part of that dream had not come true.

※

THE STREETS WERE busy on this Saturday morning, and May kept her head down as she hastened toward the doctor's practice. It felt strange to be out here alone, without Eunice or Ralph; strange, and terribly vulnerable. Already two men had wolf-whistled to her when she'd hurried past, and many more watched her with lustful and shameless eyes.

Her heart pounded uncomfortably as she reached the edge of the busy street. Ralph had somehow found a doctor willing to go into the filthy tenement buildings, but the trouble with him was that he lived half an hour's walk away, and May still had two blocks to go. She could only pray that he would come at once.

Leaving Mama alone for so long terrified her; besides, if she didn't get back to work soon, she would fail to meet the slop-shop's quota. She could only pray she would be able to work through the night somehow, and that there would be enough money left in Ralph's purse for candles. And that Mama would be well enough to take the clothing there on Monday morning. It seemed impossible, and May's stomach knotted with nervousness. If she took the clothes herself, the jig would be up. The owners would likely be furious at the deception. She would be out of a job.

And her world would fall apart.

She gazed mindlessly down the street, waiting for the traffic to clear enough for her to cross it. It was bustling here. Pedestrians, donkey carts, even a few people on horseback were hurrying to and fro. May seldom saw horses, and she found herself watching them pass with a tiny spark of joy in her heart; they were so graceful and powerful, and she remembered all the little horses she'd made for little girls back in the good days in the tenement.

The thought made tears fill her eyes. She had lost Taylor, now Ralph. Was she destined to lose every boy she loved?

A flash of black caught her eye, and she watched idly as a beautiful black horse moved up the road toward her. Its coat shimmered in the faint sunlight that was just starting to show its face between the clouds. May wondered if one could make a dress in exactly that shade of satiny black, and... but no. She didn't have other ideas. She couldn't find beauty in her heart anymore.

The horse suddenly stopped, and a deep voice spoke. "May?"

May raised her eyes, and it was *him*. It was Taylor. The soft brown eyes were his, and they were unchanged, even if everything else about him was different, even if he was wearing a warm coat and jodhpurs, even if he had a stubble of beard on his cheeks, even if his shoulders had grown broad and strong and his limbs were long and steady against his horse. Even if he was sitting astride a fine black horse and had real flesh on his bones and his cheeks were filled with colour, his eyes were *exactly the same*, soft and brown, deep and gentle, and they sparkled when they met hers.

May thought she might faint where she stood. "Taylor?" She gasped.

"May!" He flung himself down from the horse and reached his arms out toward her, coming onto the pavement. May took two staggering steps and she was in his arms at last, the way she had dreamed for so many years, the way she had despaired of ever being again.

"Oh, May, May!" Taylor was whispering, stroking her hair. "Oh, I can't believe it's really you."

May had no words. She simply clung to him, feeling his strength and substance against her, but also the familiar tenderness of his embrace. Everything had changed, and yet at the same time, nothing had changed. He was not only alive, he was *well* – and he was still Taylor, *her* Taylor, the gentle boy with the soft eyes—the boy she had loved before she knew what love truly was.

※

MAY ATE as though she had not had a bite in days, and judging by her appearance, Taylor was quite sure that had to be the case. He sat opposite her at the inn's table, ignoring the glares from the staff as her unwashed reek filled the room.

It broke his heart to see her this way; perhaps he had never realized how poor they really were, or how much better-off he was now that he was working for Mr. Goswick. She was wearing a filthy, threadbare dress that hung loosely from her bony frame, and she ate her stew in giant gulps, panting as she burned her mouth but apparently unable to slow down.

"I'm sorry," Taylor said as she looked up from the empty bowl. "I wish I could get you more, but that was my last money."

"Taylor, it was wonderful," May breathed. "Thank you." She looked faintly confused at his words, and he knew she must think it odd that he had no money, considering he was staying in a decent inn like this.

"To tell you the truth, May, I have no money at all," Taylor admitted. "Not even a job that pays anything, apart from tips." He bit his lip. "But I hope to change that. All of it."

May smiled. "It sounds like you're finally about to tell me more about what you've been doing since we were last together."

Taylor had insisted on buying her food before he would tell her anything at all. May had insisted on getting food for her mother instead, so Taylor had bought her a large loaf of bread and then the bowl of stew here at the inn. He could only imagine how desperate May was for a piece of that bread herself, but she kept it firmly in her lap, both hands resting on it as though she were afraid someone might snatch it from her. He wasn't surprised. On the walk to the inn, she had told him everything; how they had lost their tenement, and she had begun working for the slop-shop under the guise that it was Miss Eplett's work. And how Miss Eplett herself was desperately ill.

Taylor did his best to tell her his own story, trying to justify the way he had left them even though he knew it was inexcusable. But May did not seem angry. She just kept saying, "I'm so glad you're all right," making him think they had believed he had come to some grisly end. It only made him feel worse.

"... and now I've bought my horse at last," he finished. "He's young and not much to look at now, but I know I can make something of him. I'm sure of it. Then I can hire him out, and buy more horses, and build a business of my own." He reached out, laying a hand over hers. "And then I will come for you, May, if you want me to."

May's eyes shone at those words. "Oh, Taylor, I want nothing more in all the world," she breathed.

It still amazed him that those beautiful eyes would look at him like that, after all these years; as though he was the only thing in the entire world, as though he was something absolutely priceless.

"I wish I could take you with me now," he said. "How I wish I could."

"I couldn't go now, even if you could take me," May reminded him gently. "Mama is too ill. But perhaps she'll be well enough to travel soon. And I'm sure it won't be long before she's well enough to write you."

"Yes. Perhaps I can get Percy to write to you for me. He can read, and he's kind," said Taylor. "And we've told each other our addresses. So now we never have to lose each other again."

May turned her hand over, closing it over his, and his body thrilled at her touch.

"Must you go?" she whispered.

He had asked himself that same question a thousand times just in the past ten minutes, but he knew the answer. London had long since showed him that it had no opportunities for him. He had the colt now; given a year or two, he could build his business, and give May something better than she had now.

"I must," he said. "But if you are ever in trouble, have your mama write to me, and I'll come at once."

Her smile fluttered. "All right."

He knew it was the right thing, but all the same, when he left her on her way to the doctor's office with the loaf of bread clutched closely in her arms, it was all he could do not to run after her.

CHAPTER 21

THE DOCTOR'S face was blank as he withdrew the needle after giving Mama an injection of something in her arm. The sight made May shudder and turn her face away; Mama seemed far less affected. Instead, the lines of pain upon her face smoothed, and she let out a long sigh, her head leaning back against the pallet. Her hand, wrapped in May's, went dreadfully limp.

"Mama?" May gasped, tightening her grasp.

"She won't hear you now, dear," said the doctor. He was a mild-mannered, stooped little man, his long white whiskers accentuating the low droop of his lips and jowls. "This will make her sleep for some time, but it takes the pain away."

Mama did seem more peaceful; when May touched her brow, she fancied that she was a little cooler.

"Is she getting better?" May asked.

The doctor paused. "No," he said. "I'm afraid not."

He straightened, and something in his face made May's heart tremble to its core. She clutched Mama's hand a little tighter. "Sir, what's wrong with her? I thought you said it was pneumonia. I thought she would get better."

"She should be better. The medicine should have worked," said the doctor. "But I'm afraid she is quite beyond help now."

"Beyond help?" May couldn't understand.

"Yes." The doctor paused, his eyes pained. "I'm sorry, miss, but your mother is dying."

"Dying." May felt as though a bolt of lightning had been sent through her heart, even though, in the back of her mind, she knew she had been expecting it. "Why? What of? How... how does this happen?" She was trembling, tears filling her eyes.

"She's just worn out by life," said the doctor quietly. "She is spent, body and soul. I'm afraid there's nothing anyone can do for her now."

Sobs wrenched from May, and tears rushed down her cheeks. "But w-what will I do?" she sobbed. "What will I do?"

"The only thing you can do is to be with her," said the doctor. He set a large bottle of medicine on the desk; it signified the last pennies from Ralph's purse. "Give her this, as much as she will drink, to keep her comfortable. Keep her warm. Stay beside her."

The tears met beneath May's chin and ran down her throat.

"I'm truly sorry," said the doctor. He lifted his black bag and left quietly, shutting the door softly behind him.

"Oh, Mama," May whispered, gathering her mother up into her arms. "Mama, Mama, Mama."

She drowned in a tidal wave of sobbing.

TAYLOR HAD HAD his misgivings over riding back to the livery on Raven and leading, not just two quiet draft horses, but one three-year-old colt, as well. But he had made his choice well. The colt kept its head quietly beside his knee, yielded instantly to the lightest pull on the rope, and behaved impeccably all the way home.

Between that and the prospect of a letter from May and Miss Eplett sometime, Taylor was flushed with triumph when he came clattering into the livery as the late afternoon light turned to pure gold and poured over the fields. He was glad to see Mr. Goswick shuffling from the house to meet him. The old man's eyes were rheumy, and he was swathed in scarves and coats and hats, but his glowering stare had regained some of its strength as Taylor clattered into the yard.

"What is *this*?" he thundered.

Some of the other stable lads hurried up to take Raven and the draft horses. Taylor kept a firm grip on his colt; he almost didn't want to let him go, just in case he turned out not to be real after all.

"This, sir," said Taylor, beaming, "is my colt."

"Your colt," spluttered Mr. Goswick.

To pre-empt the worst of Mr. Goswick's rage, Taylor pulled out the purse he had been given and dropped it into Mr. Goswick's hands. "I paid much less for each horse than you said I could, sir, and they look good," he said. "What do you think?"

"What do I think?" shrieked Mr. Goswick. "I don't care about the draft horses. I want to know about this." He dissolved into a fit of coughing.

"Are you all right, sir?" asked Taylor.

"I would be if you would explain why this scruffy animal is in my yard."

Taylor took a deep breath. "Sir, I told you some time ago about the clients giving me tips from time to time."

"I don't care if they do," snapped Mr. Goswick.

"So this colt was going for just a pound," said Taylor. "And look at him, Mr. Goswick. He's going to be a beauty."

"A beauty?" spluttered the old man.

"I spent my own money on him, sir, don't worry," said Taylor. "Look closely. Look past his mane and his condition. Imagine him in a year, with a bit of fat, and shoes..."

Mr. Goswick was staring closely at the colt, which stretched out a nose to him and tried to lip his hand.

"He's friendly, too," said Taylor.

"How do you expect to feed and stable this animal?" Mr. Goswick snapped, turning glaring eyes back to Taylor.

Taylor hesitated. "I – I'm not sure yet," he admitted. "But I – I'll use the money I get from tips, and I'll put him in the back field where no one can see him. Oh, please, Mr. Goswick, let me put him out there. There's so much grass, much more than we really need. He'll be all right on grass. Won't he?"

Mr. Goswick sighed, but he must have seen some kind of potential in the colt. "Do as you wish," he grumbled. "Just get this awful animal out of my sight. And don't bring him back until he looks like something, do you understand?"

"Yes, sir. Thank you, sir," gasped Taylor, but Mr. Goswick was already stomping angrily back to his office, muttering.

Nonetheless, Taylor's heart thudded with hope. He was going to make this colt into something special – and then he would go to find May when he had money. Then everything would be so much better.

"May?"

The voice was a thin, feeble croak. May raised her head at once from where she was bent over her sewing. Mama was stirring on the pallet, her thin hand twitching weakly at the blanket.

"Mama." May grabbed the medicine bottle from the desk and hurried to her. "Here – drink this." She had been giving Mama this medicine as often as she was awake for the past two days, and at least the fever dreams seemed to have stopped, but her mother scarcely breathed a word to her.

"No... no," Mama breathed. She reached up, pushing away the bottle with a feeble hand.

"It's medicine, Mama. It's good for you," May whispered. "Let me give it to you."

"No... not... not yet... can't sleep now." Mama took a long, rattling breath and coughed, which ended in a moan of agony.

"Please, Mama, it'll help you."

"No... I need... a clear head." Mama blinked up at her. "I have... to tell you... about your father."

"My father?" May blinked. She supposed she must have known she had a father, but truth be told, she had never even thought of him.

"Yes," croaked Mama. "Listen... closely."

"You don't need to tell me," said May softly. "Just rest."

"No. You must... know." Mama swallowed painfully. "Your father was... Ludwig Turner."

"Oh," said May. "That's why you kept saying his name in your sleep. It makes sense now."

"Yes," croaked Mama. "But you... don't know... who the Turner family is."

"No, I don't."

Mama's face twisted in a pain that seemed to be more than just physical. "They're a rich family... live uptown. Ludwig was... the master of the house." She took a deep breath, closing her eyes, and whispered the next words. "I was the parlour-maid. And he... he was married... but..."

"Oh," said May, softly, a little startled.

"It was wrong... stupid... a young girl... looking for attention." Mama looked up at May, her eyes filled with sorrow. "But I don't... I don't regret it... not for one moment."

"But didn't it make things hard for you, when you were pregnant?" May asked.

"No... darling... Ludwig set us up in a house... a lovely house." Mama's smile flickered. "We were only... turned out... when he died."

Tears choked May's throat. "Oh, Mama, did you lose your job because of me? Did all this happen to you because of me?"

"May." Mama snatched at her hand with a sudden, desperate strength. "May, you must know something... you must know... I would do it all over again... just to have you. You were born... of my folly... but you became... my one strength."

"Mama..." May croaked. A thousand scenes of Mama's suffering filled her mind; all she had known all her life was a mother who suffered, a mother who laboured, a mother who worked desperately to give May everything she could. Of course, she'd had no small part in that labour, but she had always known – would always know – that every breath Mama drew was to care for May. Mama had never stopped trying. Never stopped fighting.

"I have... no regrets... except one." Mama's eyes filled with tears. "I wish I could... have given you... a better life."

"Mama, you love me," May sobbed. "That's more than many children ever have."

Mama's mouth trembled into a smile. "Then I can say... for one reason alone... that my life was worth living," she whispered. "That reason... my darling... was you."

"Mama, no," May whimpered.

But Mama's eyes were fluttering closed, and with a last squeeze of her hand over May's, she breathed her last.

PART VI

CHAPTER 22

Two Years Later

MAY REACHED up to rub the tiredness from around her eyes. Even in the balmy autumn sunshine pouring in from the window, her eyes felt blurry and sore when she looked down at the stitches. This was the third black woollen dress she was making this week, and it seemed to be monotony as well as strain that was making her eyes water and her fingers feel dull and stupid as they stumbled on the needle.

"What's the matter, girl?" spat an angry voice by her ear. "Would you prefer to go back to the cellar?"

May cringed, her hands working quickly, forcing her watering eyes to stay open. "No, sir," she stammered.

The shop owner, Alfred Cummings, was short and fat with a plume of unruly blond hair sprouting from above angry little black eyes that glared at her from over half-moon spectacles. Mama had told her – when she was still with her, God rest her soul – that Alfred had taken over the shop from the late Mr. Cummings Senior four or five years ago. May supposed this was a stroke of brilliant luck. The late Mr. Cummings might never have agreed to keep her on when she arrived, late, crying, and clutching a miserable half of the quota of clothes, on that black Monday after Mama died two years ago. She had begged him not only to allow her to keep working, despite her failure to meet the quota and the deception her mother had caused, but also for somewhere else to work. She had secretly hoped he would take her to the slop-workers' accommodation that the other girls and men worked in. Facing that dark cellar all on her own, when she had just weeks ago shared it with Mama and all four Glovers, was unthinkable.

Luckily for her, Alfred had overhauled the business in the years since his father had died, and it was booming. He was in no position to turn away slop-workers. Unluckily for her, his accommodations had been full. May was stuck living in the cellar.

She could work, at least, in the shop; although perhaps this position was not as enviable as she had originally hoped. Having Alfred hovering over her shoulder, constantly plying her with the same threat, had quickly grown tiresome and exhausting.

"I should hope not," Alfred growled. "I could send you back to that cellar any minute I like, you know."

"Yes, sir," said May.

"Don't you forget it." Alfred stamped off back to the shop floor, and May ducked her head, reminding herself that she was grateful for sunlight.

She kept working, her callused fingers gripping the needle tightly; she almost didn't feel the pain anymore if she pricked herself or pressed too hard. By the end of the day, the skirt was finished, and May's voice felt cracked and tired from disuse. Alfred wouldn't let her sing or hum, and he wasn't in favour of chitchat in the slop-shop.

The one thing there was, however, was paper. She shared a space with stacks of old papers and files and books, and Alfred didn't seem to mind if she took pieces of paper from the rubbish bin. It was easier than disposing of it himself, May supposed. She hung up the finished dress and slipped the precious piece of paper from the drawer of the real desk she was now working on. It was folded in half, and she opened it just a bit, just enough to glimpse the design she'd drawn there.

It had been life-changing to find out that there was a person in the slop-shop who was solely responsible for drawing the patterns that May had been making for so many years. She was an elderly woman who was also responsible for cooking Alfred's lunch, and she was as stodgy and tasteless as both her designs and her pottage. May felt a flutter of excitement as she clutched her design in one hand and pulled on her coat with the other. Surely Alfred would see that if they could make their clothes a little more interesting, more people would want them.

She passed by his office on the way out of the shop; it was closed and long since dark, and Alfred seemed ready to leave himself. He was getting up from his desk and reaching for his coat.

"Sir, may I trouble you?" May asked.

"No," said Alfred shortly, shrugging on his coat.

"Sir, I just wanted to show you something." May unfolded the design and held it out. "Don't you think our tailcoats would sell better if we made them like this? Ours are really quite old-fashioned, and – "

"Just shut up and do your sewing, girl," spat Alfred, shouldering past her. "Now get out. I want to lock the shop."

May felt everything within her cry out at his harsh words. She wondered, not for the first time, what was wrong with her. Why was it that everything she considered beautiful was stupid in the eyes of everyone else? Why was the world so harsh in rejecting her efforts to make it a slightly softer, slightly kinder, slightly lovelier place?

THE RAGGED SEAMSTRESS

She blinked back her tears, ducked her head and hurried out of the shop and into the black streets. Bitter cold seeped up from the ground like some vengeful spirit bent on shrinking and destroying any flesh it found. She turned up the collar of her coat, sinking down into it. She'd made it herself; it had broken her heart to find, now that she no longer had to pay for candles or feed Mama, she could afford her own clothes. She would a thousand times over rather have had Mama than the nicest clothes in the world.

The nicest clothes in the world... She tipped back her head, taking a fresh breath of the cold night air, and allowed herself to dream of the shop she would own someday. It would be called Blanche Fashion, and she would make the most beautiful things there. Dresses she had only ever dreamed of. Beautiful, flowing, white wedding gowns like the queen's. Exotic ballgowns that would turn heads across even the biggest and most lavish of ballrooms. They would all come from May's hands, and she would draw the designs for them, and a team of happy, well-fed young seamstresses would make them. Seamstresses who would learn the art of design themselves, and grow up into better lives someday...

Arriving at her cellar took a needle to the balloon of her dream; it burst and disappeared with a bang that shook her. She pushed the door open and stepped into the darkness, groping in the niche for her candle. A part of her soul always expected Mama to be waiting here when she lit the candle, sitting on the pallet, laughing. But Mama wasn't here. Mama was long gone and buried in a pauper's grave which May could not so much as visit.

There was just the bare walls of the cellar. And when May lowered the candle to peer at the threshold, there were no letters there, either.

Part of her had hoped Ralph might write. She had been so tempted to find him after Mama died, but then the letter from Taylor had come. May had been unable to read a word of the fine scrawl – Percy's, she assumed – except for her own name. Without Mama, she was crippled. Yet the letter had given her hope; and she had no way of telling Taylor where she was if she moved from the cellar. It was that knowledge that had kept her down here in the dark for the past two years.

She sat down on the pallet, resting her aching feet for a moment. Taylor had come to see her once or twice, but not at all in the last year. And for the past six months, there had been no letters.

Perhaps he had forgotten her. Perhaps the whole world had forgotten her.

Perhaps even the brightest candle could be snuffed out by the rising darkness.

CHAPTER 23

TAYLOR FELT that his heart could burst as he watched the young gelding trot into the yard. He could hardly believe that it was the same horse he had bought on that London livestock sale two years ago. The gangly three-year-old had fleshed out into a beautiful, strong five-year-old with enormous, ground-eating paces; his ugly, patchy grey coat was now a shimmering dappled grey, his mane cloud-white upon his neck. But the eye was as gentle as it had always been, and that was what made Future as popular with ladies as with men.

It was a lady riding him side-saddle now, accompanied by a young gentleman on Raven, and her cheeks were flushed with pleasure, eyes shining.

"Good afternoon, ma'am." said Taylor, taking Future's rein as she dismounted. "Did you have a good ride?"

"Oh, my dear sir, a wonderful ride," she said.

"The last livery horse we hired threw her and shook her very badly," said the gentleman. "That was why I asked for your gentlest horse this morning, and I was rather surprised when you suggested this youngster. But he didn't put a foot wrong all day. Why, Miranda here was even galloping and jumping hedges by the end of it, laughing all the way."

"He's quite given me my joy back when it comes to riding," beamed the lady. "I must thank Mr. Goswick. Is he here?"

"I'm afraid not, ma'am," said Taylor, "but I'll be sure to pass on the message."

Stable lads took the horses off to their stables as Taylor accepted the money. He took it into the office and locked it neatly in the safe, then tucked the key into his pocket. Checking his new brass pocket-watch, he saw that it was almost noon. Time for Mr. Goswick's medicine.

Mounting the steps to the small flat over the stable office, Taylor entered the kitchen. The part-time cook who made Mr. Goswick's meals, as well as those of the stable lads, had left a sandwich on the table for him. Taylor collected the plate as well as a glass of brandy and the bottle of medicine, then carried them all through to the bedroom.

Mr. Goswick was lying propped up on his pillows, looking out through the window over the back fields. A mare was grazing there, her foal gambolling by her side.

The foal was older now, with a thick, furry coat, but its voice was still high-pitched and playful as it bucked and kicked.

"Why haven't you weaned that blasted foal yet, Harris?" grumbled Mr. Goswick. "It's far too big to be with its dam. You'll ruin the poor mare for the whole winter at this rate."

"It's on my list for next week, Mr. Goswick," said Taylor patiently.

"List. List. Do it now, boy." the old man spluttered, and then began to cough, a painful sound like wet leather being dragged over gravel. Taylor hastily set the plate down on the nightstand and offered Mr. Goswick the brandy. He drank it off at a gulp, then fell back against his pillows, panting. His lips were ringed with blue.

"Are you all right, sir?" Taylor asked.

"I'm dying, boy," Mr. Goswick groaned.

The news had come a year ago, and Taylor still wasn't used to it. Yet when his eyes dwelled on the deep hollows of Mr. Goswick's skull and the pitiful weakness of his trembling hands as he clutched the glass, he knew that the end could not be far.

"Your medicine, sir," he said, holding up the bottle.

Mr. Goswick shook the bottle and grimaced at the sight of it. "Ghastly stuff," he grumbled. "If the doctor wants to kill me, he should put a bullet in my head like an old horse. Would be kinder."

"Don't say that, sir," said Taylor. "Here are some ham sandwiches for you."

"Ham sandwiches. Fine food for a dying man, ham sandwiches," grumbled Mr. Goswick.

Taylor knew that life was becoming unutterably lonely for the bedridden old man up here in his flat. He didn't know why Mr. Goswick didn't have any family, but he assumed he did not; if there were other Goswicks, surely, they would be the ones feeding and tending him, sending for the doctor, making sure he took his medicine, running the livery yard instead of Taylor.

"Future went out with a nervous lady today," he said. "He was wonderful. The lady was grinning all over her face when they came back."

Some of the old gleam returned to Mr. Goswick's eyes at that. "I told you that horse would be something, boy," he rasped.

"He really is," said Taylor proudly. "It won't be long before I can buy myself another and grow my little business."

Mr. Goswick grunted. "A fine time of it you're having, trying to grow your own business while running after some sickly old man," he said.

Taylor glanced at him, surprised at the words. It was perhaps the first time he had ever heard any kind of empathy in Mr. Goswick's voice. But the old man seemed to be in a strange mood. He was watching the foal, which had grown tired of its antics and folded up in the autumn grass to sleep.

"Don't be alone," he said suddenly. "Never grow into a crotchety old man all on your own, boy. Never."

"You're not alone, sir," said Taylor.

Mr. Goswick snorted. "Stable lads don't count," he said. Looking up at Taylor, he had a sudden urgency in his voice. "Promise me, boy. Promise me you won't be alone all your life."

A spasm of familiar longing rushed through Taylor's body. He lowered his eyes, thinking of the letters he'd been writing to May, letters that never had an answer. He knew why, of course; with Miss Eplett gone, May couldn't write back, nor even read the letters. Still, at their last visit, she'd told him they brought her solace. Just knowing that he remembered her made her feel better.

The thought of her working away day in and day out, returning every night to that dark cellar, was a horrific lead burden that Taylor struggled to carry. It was why he was so glad that Future was doing well, that his savings were adding up. He prayed that soon it would be enough for him to see May more often, if not to bring her here and marry her the way he wished. If only he could visit her. His last trip had been in spring; winter was rapidly approaching now. But Mr. Goswick needed him.

"Promise me." There was a trembling urgency in Mr. Goswick's voice.

"I promise," said Taylor quietly. "There is someone... already. I won't be alone."

Mr. Goswick seemed mollified. He sank back onto his pillows. "Good," he whispered, and the ache of loneliness in that word seemed more than one syllable could bear.

⁂

That was the last word Mr. Goswick spoke.

Taylor knew, that evening, the moment he rode in from exercising one of the hunters in preparation for the winter and saw Percy's face where the head lad stood in the yard. The chubby man's skin was a terrible pallid grey, and his hands trembled where he clutched a stable rubber in them, wringing it this way and that as though he could wring the joy out of it.

"Percy?" Taylor flung himself down from the sweaty hunter. "What is it?"

"It's – it's Mr. Goswick." Percy's fat face crumpled and reddened. "He's gone. He's gone, Taylor, he's gone."

Taylor's heart froze within him, and with a sudden stab of agony he realized that he wasn't ready to lose Mr. Goswick.

Not the stable yard, not his job – but Mr. Goswick himself. His heart thudded, and he flung the reins at the nearest stable lad and rushed through the office and up the stairs.

He almost bowled over the doctor, who was standing in the kitchen, his hat in one hand, the other resting on the knob of the bedroom door as though he had just closed it. When he saw the question written on Taylor's face, he bowed his head.

"I'm sorry, son," he said. "Mr. Goswick is gone; went off peacefully in his sleep, by the looks of it."

Taylor felt his knees had turned to water. He sank into one of the chairs by the kitchen table, lowering his head into his hands. Mr. Goswick had been a bully, had never had a good word to say to anyone, but he had nonetheless been there for so many years of Taylor's life that it seemed impossible for him to be gone. A sick realization washed over him. What would happen to him now? The livery yard would be sold, auctioned off... Where would he go? Where would he take Future? How would he feed them both?

Grief and terror overwhelmed him in waves. The doctor put a hand on his shoulder. "You know, Mr. Goswick was lonely all his life," he said, "but you were a son to him."

Taylor raised his head, startled to hear this, but the doctor was already stepping out of the kitchen. The door had barely closed behind him when Percy came in. There were frank tears glimmering on his cheeks; the man brushed them away quickly before coming to stand in front of Taylor. He had replaced the stable rubber with his cap, which creaked as he wrung it in both hands.

"Mr. Taylor, sir," he said, "there's something Mr. Goswick wanted me to tell you as soon as he died."

Taylor blinked. *Mr. Taylor, sir?* Percy had never called him that. Percy was his superior, after all, as was almost everyone else on the yard. The poor man's brains must be scrambled by the shock of Mr. Goswick's death.

"What is it, Percy?" he asked.

Percy took a deep breath. "Mr. Goswick was never married, never had any children, as you know, sir," he said. "But he did leave a will... left it with his solicitor, he says. He told me what was in it. He wanted me to be the one to tell you, not some stranger."

Taylor sat up, fear filling him. Was this about Future? Was Mr. Goswick going to claim him, the only thing Taylor owned?

"What?" he croaked, with a dry mouth.

"Taylor, Mr. Goswick left everything to one person. Just one." Percy seemed to be groping for words.

"What?" said Taylor. "Who?" A beat of hope surged in his heart. If it was Percy, then he knew he would be treated kindly.

Percy bit his lip.

"You," Percy said.

Taylor stared at him. For an instant the world froze; then the walls of the room seemed to spin around him, and he had to shake his head rapidly to clear the dizzy feeling.

"What? No," he said. "It can't be. Why – why – what...?" His words seemed to have dried up; all coherency had left his mind, replaced with a senseless buzz.

"He loved you from the moment you led Spark back and advocated for her the day that boy took her out," said Percy softly. "He may never have showed it, but you became his son that day, and he only grew to love you more and more as you worked on the yard."

"But... but..." Taylor stammered. "He... he was so unkind..." He stopped. The truth was that Mr. Goswick had been unkind, but only in his words; he had always given Taylor what he needed, always provided more chances than Taylor had ever dreamed of.

"He didn't know how to love anymore," said Percy softly. "He had no wife to teach him how. But he did his best for you."

Taylor realized that there were tears on his cheeks. "Percy, it should be you. You've been working for him all your life."

"Oh, no, sir." Percy's eyes widened. "I don't want nothing to do with managing this place. Head lad – that's my place. There's a good pension, and my wife and kids are happy, and that's all I want. Oh, no, sir, you can have it."

You can have it. Taylor looked out of the kitchen window, over the stable yard full of horses. Over the dream that had just come true for him.

"It's yours, sir," said Percy. "It's all yours."

The reality hit him like a warm wave to the chest.

"This – this is – this is everything I've ever dreamed of," he gasped. "Oh – thank God. Thank God." He surged to his feet, grabbing Percy's arms. "Percy, I have to go."

"Go?" questioned Percy. "Where?"

"London," cried Taylor, running for the kitchen door.

"London? Sir? Sir," Percy cried after him.

"I'll be back tonight." Taylor shouted over his shoulder, running down the stairs. "I'll be back."

And this time, May would be with him.

EPILOGUE

Six Years Later

Yours sincerely,

Eunice.

May smiled, folding the letter up again and setting it down on her desk. It lay among the mad chaos of her desk: drawings, bits of fabric, and scraps of ribbon lay everywhere, strewn willy-nilly all over her small office. There was an easel in the corner, a half-finished design upon it.

Humming to herself, May turned back to the easel and started to work with long sweeps of her pencil, adding a sweetheart neckline to the dress she was designing. She cocked her head to one side, inspecting it. Was it quite right? Perhaps it was a little too girlish for this bride. She was a widow, and this was her second marriage, after all. Yet perhaps she wanted to feel innocent and free again on her wedding day. May added a few more experimental strokes of her pencil.

There was a tap at the office door. "Mrs. Harris?" said a nervous little voice.

May got up to open the door, smiling down at a nervous young face. The girl's cheeks were far rounder these days, she noticed, and her newfound colour was bringing out the freckles that pallor and emaciation had hidden when she'd first come to work for May two months ago.

"What is it, Eva?" she asked.

"You asked me to tell you when Mr. Harris came back from the hunt, ma'am," said Eva.

"Oh, wonderful. Is he here?"

"He is, ma'am."

"Good girl. You and Rose can look after the shop for an hour, now." May stepped out of her office. "I'm riding out with my family. It's such a nice day."

"Yes, ma'am," said the little seamstress, following May as she stepped onto the floor of her little millinery. A smile lifted her lips as soon as she did so. There were only a few mannequins standing about, displaying some of May's favorite pieces: a plum-coloured suit with a top hat whose bright yellow ribbon perfectly complemented the daffodil in its buttonhole; a glorious ballgown every colour of water, flowing like a stream; a neat riding suit for a lady, with its sturdy tweed skirt and well-cut jacket. There were flowers arranged all around her. The architect had thought she and Taylor were crazy when she had insisted on the largest windows possible, but with sunlight streaming into the room, May did not regret it.

She took a deep, happy breath, nodded to the girl behind the counter, and stepped out of the millinery and under the sign that read *Blanche Fashion* above her head. In a few strides, she had walked into the stable yard. Having the millinery on the same property as the yard had proven to be wildly successful; it seemed that people hiring horses had the money for good clothes, too.

"Mama," squealed a delighted little voice, and a round-cheeked boy ran across the yard toward her, holding out his arms.

"Quincy." May swept him into her arms and spun him around. The little boy had Taylor's dark eyes, but her mother's soft blonde hair. May kissed both his cheeks. "Are you ready to ride?"

"Pony ride. Pony ride," squealed Quincy.

"He's growing up to be a horseman like his father, Mrs. Harris," chuckled stout old Percy, leading Quincy's saddled pony onto the yard.

"He certainly is. Although perhaps I did hope he would be a tailor instead," smiled May. She settled the boy into the pony's saddle.

"Perhaps the next one will be, my dear," boomed Taylor's voice.

May turned. He was striding toward her, pleasantly sweaty, his cheeks coloured, his eyes bright and shining and yet as gentle as ever. He threw an arm around her and kissed her with abandon so that she giggled like a girl.

"Sir," protested Percy, blushing.

"Oh, before I forget to tell you, darling," said May, "Eunice wrote to us. She says that she and Ralph and his wife would love to stay for Christmas, as you suggested."

"Wonderful," said Taylor.

Two other stable lads had brought out their horses. Taylor had chosen the ever-well-behaved Raven, as he would be leading Quincy. He only ever allowed May to ride Future. Although the big gelding had lost his dapples to age and begun to turn almost white, May still thought he was as beautiful as he had been the day that Taylor came galloping up to the slop-shop in a fine fury, calling her name.

Everything had changed for her on that day in London, six years ago.

"Ready, my darling?" Taylor asked her.

She smiled up into his eyes. With him beside her, she was ready for whatever life had in store for them next.

The End

CONTINUE READING...

Thank you for reading *The Ragged Seamstress!* Are you wondering what to read next? Why not read ***The Fraudulent Governess?*** **Here's a sneak peek for you:**

Sophia Morgan's scream echoed around the lavish furnishings of her room, a hoarse, animal sound of pain and desperation. Her body tensed in a long, trembling contraction, the bulge of her belly tightening, misshapen under the front of her wrapper. The lower part of the wrapper was unbuttoned, her bare knees jutting shockingly from among the mess of fabric. Elsie Carter had never seen so much of Sophia's skin before. She doubted anyone had, except for Master Simon, but Master Simon was all the way in India now, and he had no idea his first child was coming into the world in the middle of a blizzard.

Sophia's scream and contraction eased at the same time, and she fell back against her sumptuous silk pillows, her sweat-soaked black hair fanning out around her. Her usually porcelain-perfect complexion was blotched with red, and her eyes were desperate as she stared up at Elsie.

"He's coming. He's coming," she panted. "I can't keep him inside."

"Don't try," said Elsie. "Everything is going to be all right." She tried to keep the tremor out of her own voice as she said it.

"All right?" Sophia sobbed with angry sarcasm. "How can it be all right? The snow is three feet deep. There's no calling a midwife, there's no calling a doctor, my mother is long dead, my mother-in-law is frail..." She led out a moan, her head tossing on the pillow. "I'm delivering my baby all alone."

Sophia's hands were lying in bunched fists on the bed on either side of her, and on an impulse, Elsie reached out and wrapped her fingers around one of them. She knew that it was unthinkable for a mere lady's maid to touch her mistress in such a manner, but she also knew Sophia was terrified, and she empathized powerfully with that terror.

"You're not alone, ma'am," she said.

Sophia gave her a desperate look. "What do you know about delivering babies?" She panted, her body shaking as another contraction came for her.

"I delivered my own just a few weeks ago, remember?" said Elsie, managing a smile. Unlike Sophia, she *had* been truly alone, and it had been the most terrifying experience of her life. But she had survived. And so would Sophia, she prayed.

There was no time for further speculation. Sophia let out another shriek of agony, and the piercing sound woke Elsie's baby where she lay wrapped in blankets on the sofa where Elsie had hastily put her down when she'd seen Sophia's sodden bedclothes and known that the baby was coming. Elsie was forced to ignore little Ada's cries as she reached for the young life that was coming into the world, the tiny face squeezing out into the cold air.

"Push, Sophia," she shouted. "The baby's almost here. Push. *Push.*"

Click Here to Continue Reading!

https://www.ticahousepublishing.com/victorian-romance.html

THANKS FOR READING

If you love Victorian Romance, **Click Here**

https://victorian.subscribemenow.com/

to hear about all **New Faye Godwin Romance Releases! I will let you know as soon as they become available!**

Thank you, Friends! If you enjoyed *The Ragged Seamstress,* would you kindly take a couple minutes to leave a positive review on Amazon? It only takes a moment, and positive reviews truly make a difference. Thank you so much! I appreciate it!

Much love,

Faye Godwin

MORE FAYE GODWIN VICTORIAN ROMANCES!

We love rich, dramatic Victorian Romances and have a library of Faye Godwin titles just for you! (Remember that ALL of Faye's Victorian titles can be downloaded FREE with Kindle Unlimited!)

CLICK HERE to discover Faye's Complete Collection of Victorian Romance!
https://ticahousepublishing.com/victorian-romance.html

ABOUT THE AUTHOR

Faye Godwin has been fascinated with Victorian Romance since she was a teen. After reading every Victorian Romance in her public library, she decided to start writing them herself —which she's been doing ever since. Faye lives with her husband and young son in England. She loves to travel throughout her country, dreaming up new plots for her romances. She's delighted to join the Tica House Publishing family and looks forward to getting to know her readers.

contact@ticahousepublishing.com

Printed in Great Britain
by Amazon